Plight

Journey of a Brooklyn soldier

This book is a story about my life. My struggles, hurts and pains. When you read this, I hope it touches you in the deep depths of your heart and to the core of your very soul. I pray it's like a self-help book to you. My mistakes should be your guidelines. Walk with me in a first-person (POV) experience and see the world through my eyes.

Intro!

I knew I had a serious problem when I grabbed her neck for the first time. What's worse is, I don't even remember why I did it. The only thing I can recall is the woman I called "mine" getting me upset and me tossing her across the room by her neck. Although I wasn't new to that, this was the first time I felt the need to seek help, professional help. There were several other women who have seen that side of me. Whether it was choking them with their own scarves or holding their breaths, the fact remains that I had an abusive history. What was wrong with me? Why was I so angry? I mean, I did have a conscience and I wasn't heartless. I was even remorseful after I calmed down. After hitting the floor, Kenniya looked at me with such sadness in her eyes. Her gaze had a mixture of shock and hurt but love was still there. We looked at each other for five seconds realizing that I broke my promise, my promise to never hurt her in any way. I walked over to where she was awkwardly sitting and said *"see?" "See what you made me do?"* As if it was her fault that I just choked her.

Disclaimer

The characters, events, and settings depicted in this book are entirely fictional and are not intended to represent any real individuals, organizations, or events. Any resemblance to actual persons, living or dead, or actual events is purely coincidental and unintended. The author has taken creative liberties to craft a unique narrative and setting, and any similarity to real individuals or situations is beyond the author's control. This book is a work of fiction, and readers should not assume that any events, characters or settings are based on real events or people.

Table of the Contents

Chapter 1 .... *7*

Her name is Kenniya 7

Chapter 2 .... *12*

Shawn Harris 12

Chapter 3 .... *16*

The road out 16

Chapter 4 .... *20*

Unruly 20

Chapter 5 .... *24*

What's done in the dark... 24

Chapter 6 .... *29*

Birthday Madness 29

Chapter 7 .... *35*

When I was a boy, I thought like a boy 35

Chapter 8 .... *42*

Truth is the only safe ground to stand on 42

Chapter 9 .... *49*

Bad Blood 49

Chapter 10 .... *54*

Old habits die hard 54

Chapter 11 .... *60*

Be careful what you wish for 60

Chapter 12 .... *65*

The bed defiled 65

Chapter 13 .... *69*

Impudence 69

Chapter 14 .... *73*

Calamity 73

Chapter 15 .... *78*

Forbidden Fruit 78

Chapter 16 .... *83*

Damaged Goods 83

Chapter 17 .... *87*

Typhoon 87

Chapter 18 .... *91*

The storm within 91

Chapter 19 .... *94*

Bitter Sweet 94

Chapter 20 .... *98*

A hard head makes a soft ass 98

Dedication *101*

Chapter 1

Her name is Kenniya

Her name was Kenniya Johnson. Southern born with Caribbean background. Her face was young and angelic like. She was gorgeous enough to be a model, with her big voluptuous lips and honey eyes. She was 22, about 5"3 and 127lbs. For her height, she had legs that climbed for days with a scar on the left one that showed her perfection. Her skin was that of cocoa butter, light, smooth and delicate. She had a slender physique and for her petite figure, she had ass for her size. To top it all off, she had a handful of supple breasts. We met on social media around the end of winter. One of my colleagues was showing a picture to our peers of a female he claimed he was talking to. My curiosity brought me over to where he and the others were standing. When the phone rotated to me, I studied the image that was on the screen and nodded in approval. I asked him if she has a sister and he told me "yeah" while pulling up the sister's social media profile. This time the screen showed a much prettier girl. I immediately wanted this girl for myself so I asked for her name so I could find her and send her a message. One of the other guys also wanted her so he decided to just send her a friend request. While smirking inwardly, I thought to myself "*game on*". The message I sent was a little cheesy but seemingly genuine. Not only that, I also sent it to several other females on the site. Yes, the same exact message, word for word. The message read.

> *"I'm not going to beat around the bush...I know that you hear it all the time but I've seen your picture and find you to be a very attractive*

young lady. I'm curious to see if your heart is as beautiful as you. So, if you are any kind of interested, here is my number 718-476-

8892".

She responded two days later saying that she had seen my message but somehow it was deleted.

> *Kenniya: I got your message but only for it to*
>
> *disappear.*
>
> *Shawn: Is that the reason why you haven't*
>
> *called or texted me yet? Kenniya: I didn't get any message with a number.*
>
> *Shawn: Wow...lol...Well here it is again 718-476-8892.*
>
> *Kenniya: Lol Ok. I'll call you as soon as I get*
>
> *home so I hope you're not busy for the rest of the night.*
>
> *Shawn: I'll be waiting.*

She called later that day and we had to enjoy each other's conversation because we talked for hours. It went on like that, every day for a week straight. Talking about anything and everything we could. It was apparent that we liked each other, so the only thing left for us to do was to meet. The opportunity came up when her plans for hanging out with her friends were canceled. "Perfect" I said to myself, figuring she would come spend time with me instead. I told her of my idea, and she was just as excited as I was. She asked if I wanted her to come for the day or the weekend. Kenniya lived in Trenton, NJ so I had to meet her at Penn station. She arrived at 34th st before me and the plan was that if she got there ahead of our scheduled time, that she was to wait for me at Mc Donald's. I had white tennis shoes, blue-ish jeans, a fitted under shirt and a white & blue button down over it. I also had a gym bag with extra clothes for the night. I walked inside Mc Donald's to find Kenniya waiting for me upstairs. I walked over with a smile on my face, noticing that she looked just as good in person. She wore blue overalls and white sneakers. We exchanged greetings, then I took the suitcase that she had with her and led her out the Mc Donald's to the train station. At the time, I did not live alone so I took her to a hotel. I told her of our plans for the night so she could figure out what she wanted to wear. After unpacking, she chose a dress and laid it out across the bed. The dress was mostly black, with a pink and white checkered pattern at the top. Kenniya got in the shower while I watched T.V. I went in after her but when I tried to close the door, she said *"that wasn't necessary"*. *"Oh snap"*, I thought. I came out and got dressed in front of her, thinking if I didn't need to close the bathroom door then she would not mind this either. I wore a light blue button-down shirt, blue jeans, Air Max sneakers and a fitted hat to complete my outfit. Since she said she had never been to Benihana's, I decided to take her there for dinner. We arrived at the restaurant around 9:00pm and since it was the weekend, the place was full. It was a decent size. It had stairs that led to the entrance, a small lobby and a hostess nearby to greet you. Benihana's was set up differently from most restaurants. Instead of sitting at a table with you and whoever you were with, you sat in a letter "U" formation with other people. On top of that there was a grill in the middle, where they would cook the food in front of you. The set up was interpersonal because the chef would do tricks while he was cooking. I've been there before so I knew Kenniya would enjoy herself. We stayed there for about an hour; conversing, eating and drinking. Somewhere during our conversation, I leaned over and kissed her shoulder, she then looked at me, as if to say, *"it's about to go down"*. The chemistry between us was undeniable. Two people couldn't get more comfortable with each other. After dinner we went back to the hotel. I know we had the same thing in mind because the room was thick with raging hormones and every breath of it was intoxicating. We got undressed so we could get into bed with thoughts of what was to come. I turned on the T.V. knowing that at any minute, it would be watching us. Kenniya loved to cuddle so by the time we laid down, she was already finding her way to me. The smell of her fragrance enticed me and her body brought a rise out of me. Her head was buried in my chest while I laid on my back, so I was able to run my hand up and down her curves. Her knee rested on my thigh and every time my hand grazed her skin; her body moved in unison. I turned my face to meet Hers, then I slowly leaned in, formally introducing our lips for the first time. We tasted each other's lips, briefly sucking on the fullness of each one. Then our tongues met next. After their initial greetings, our tongues played tag, wrestled a little and danced for the rest of the time. My hand slid down her curves to find her soft back side. She put her hand on my cheek, making the kiss more intimate than it was. I started rubbing on her thigh that still rested on my leg and then in one quick motion, I pulled her on top of me. She sat up to take off her dress, exposing her lovely breasts. We switched places so I could taste the nectar that was secreting from her pussy. I took off her black lace panties, spread her legs and French kissed her vulva. Every moan that escaped her lips was followed by a thrust of her pelvis. I licked on her outer lips, sucked on her inner lips, tongue punched her clit then allowed it to slide in her tight hole, making sure I lapped up every drop of her. I held on to her thighs and she held onto the back of my head. I couldn't get enough of the sweet and delicious juices that flowed in my mouth. I then rose to kiss her stomach, breasts and neck; lingering long enough to hear every reaction. She passionately kissed me, and I knew she wanted me bad because she reached down to grab my rock-hard dick. Next, she guided me to her throbbing pussy. Upon penetration, she moaned, then wrapped her legs around me, while lifting her pelvis to accept all of me. Each stroke made the room echo with the sounds of her delight. Our bodies mingled and fused until we became one entity, one being, combining our souls. We came at the same time, looking at each other with pure ecstasy in our eyes. All I could think was *"what a night"*.

Chapter 2

Shawn Harris

I was born April 24, 1988 in Brooklyn East New York. I lived in a two-family home surrounded by craziness. Although, I didn't live in the projects, my neighborhood was what you would call "ghetto". Have you ever watched the movie called "New Jack City?" Well, that was kind of how my neighborhood looked. Gangs, crack bottles as well as syringes all over the place and crack heads nearby, doing what they do best. There were also occasional "drive by's". My family was blessed because even though all of this surrounded my family of nine, not one of us has touched or put a crack pipe to our mouths or shot a needle into our veins. I have five older sisters and one younger brother; not including the three that my father has outside of his marriage. Growing up, my father was back and forth between two houses, between two women. Eventually, my father ended up staying with us more because there was no order in our house. We fought each other in the street, the house, at school and even when we went to visit family. We were out of control. My father wasn't the most loving father but when he was around, we didn't act up as much. He was stern, surly, scary and violent. I remember going to his mistress apartment and where he worked, just to get a whooping. What made it worse, was that my father was crazy, so when he used to beat us, (what he called discipline) he would whistle. He had this paddle, a wide, wooden, racquetball paddle. He would make us pull down our pants to expose our bare skin and basically swing the paddle in connection of our behinds. There was a day that my siblings and I got in trouble, down to my baby brother. He started with just lightly tapping my baby brother on the butt but the older we were, the harder his hits were as well. I remember crying in the bathroom and my sister Valerie soothing me, telling me that *"it's alright"*. In some ways, we needed to be disciplined still, not as severe as he did it. When you think about it, it was his fault because he wasn't always around. He exposed us to his infidelity and to the outcome of his affair, which was our baby sister. For some reason he was the hardest on me. I wonder if it was because I was the least obedient, the black sheep of the family or maybe because I looked exactly like him. Anyway, when it came to me, the paddle became a weapon of war. He swung it as if to injure me. There were a couple of times that the paddle struck my face and I bled so much that my white shirt ended up a totally different color. Where was my mother through it all? Right in the kitchen, smoking Salem one hundred lights. It's funny because no matter how sorry she was for allowing my dad to beat my ass, she called him whenever I got in trouble, knowing what he would do. I used to beg my mother not to tell my father when I got in trouble though a lot of times, she would tell him anyway. There were times where getting a phone call from school was the worst feeling in the world. The teacher would call my mother and tell her what devious and mischievous thing I did for the day. In return, my mother would tell my dad and the rest of the day, my heart would race, my stomach would digest itself and my intestines would be in knots. I knew the whooping would come, the only thing was, I didn't know when. My father is the type that would wait for you to take a shower and beat you with a belt. He was the type of person that at three in the morning, while you were sleeping, he was playing tag with a 2 by 4 made of wood. One day, I think my brother and I were fighting and like usual, my mother told my father. We knew that we were in for it and like usual, we didn't know when. It was the wee hours of the morning; the sun wasn't even up yet. My brother and I were dead to the world. The house was old so our floors would creak, whenever someone would walk the stairs or move throughout the house. I heard the door open and I heard my father's footsteps creak over to where I was sleeping. The only thing was, I could not get up or move. I felt the 2 by 4 hit me repeatedly in my back, shoulder, arms and legs. After he was satisfied, he crept over to my brother but my brother must have heard my screams because he was waking up. Still half asleep, my brother was rubbing his eyes trying to peer through the dark. My father immediately hid the 2 by 4 behind his back and told my brother to go back to sleep. I guess my brother sensed something was wrong or that his ass whooping had arrived because he wouldn't lay back down. So, when my father saw that his efforts of putting my brother back to sleep wasn't working, he began beating on him. I could hear the screams of my brother's agony from each time the wood made contact with my brother's body. All I could do was sit and watch in horror as I cried from my own pains. When my father was done, he left the same way he came, quietly, in the dark with nothing to be heard but the cries of freshly beaten kids and his footsteps. You think that I would learn from the beatings but boy was I a glutton for punishment. I stayed in trouble. It got to the point where my mother called the principal by his first name. She had to go to my school so many times, they asked her to be a member on the school board. What the hell was I doing in trouble in elementary school anyway? Remember food fights? I used to start them. I would pick up a milk carton, open it up, then toss it across the room to hit some poor kid in their head. The milk would splatter and soak their clothes, while also wetting anyone that was nearby. Next thing I knew, the whole cafeteria would throw anything they could pick up or the contents that were on their tray. I did that all the way up until the 7th grade. I used to make spit paper balls and make slingshots out of rubber bands. I would make paper bullets and sling them at the back of exposed necks. Pow! Do you remember cutting school in elementary? You probably don't because I was the only one doing that. I would take the metro-card and swipe someone into the turnstile and ask for their token as payment. That was how I would eat during the day. The token was $1.50 and when you exchanged it at the store, you got $1.25. I would buy zebra cakes, strawberry shortcakes and chips to feast on until I went home. I would hide in the cupboards of the school and get a kick out of knowing that no one knew where I was. I would wait until the halls were clear then pull the fire alarm and run back to my hiding spot watching all the kids line up to go outside. They would form up in their prospective classes, waiting for the fire department to check the school. I also loved playing with fire at the time. I burned everything, from spider webs to dumpsters. My brother and I almost became victims of my obsession with fire. There was this auto shop down the street from my house and right next to it was a small car lot. Cars piled on top of each other making it a mountain of fun for me. One day, I brought my brother along to play with me. We jumped from the top cars to the bottom ones then climbed back up again. We would pretend to drive each one as we went. We decided to rest for a while, so we sat in the car that was at the very top. I was on the driver's side and my brother was in the passenger seat. While he sat next to me talking about nothing, I was pulling out a book of matches from my pocket. For some reason I thought it was a good idea to take a match and burn the ceiling of the car. In a matter of seconds, the car was engulfed in flames. I could see the terror in my brother's eyes as the fire surrounded the car. Somehow, I managed to keep calm, climb out, then pull my brother out. As soon as we climbed out of the lot and our feet hit the floor, we ran as fast as our feet would let us. When we got to our house, I tried to get my breathing under control and get my brother to relax. He wasn't freaking out or anything like that but I had to make us look as non-suspicious as possible. When we finally walked in the house, one of my sister's asked *"why does it smell like smoke?"* Shortly after, we heard fire trucks outside the window. My mother questioned where our whereabouts were but after quick short answers, she let us shower and eat. Thankfully, no one was hurt because it could have gone a lot worse. I wondered if my obsession with fire resonated with my feelings at the time. Destructive in nature. GOD willing something changes before it consumes me.

Chapter 3

The road out

As a kid, I always kept my circle small. I knew a lot of people but who I considered a friend was limited. There was Malik, Jamal, Roman, Julian, Derek, Watson and Warren. Although a few others were around, these were the ones that played big roles in my life. Now Derek and I went to the same elementary school. In school Derek was popular since he played for the school's basketball team. Pretty much everybody knew him. I was just as popular but in a different way. My name was called on the intercom almost as much as the daily announcements. You would hear some random report, followed by *"Shawn Harris, please come to the principal office"*. Unlike me, Derek lived near the school in a community called Starrett City. Most of the kids that went to our school lived there. As we got older, Derek kept in touch with our peers, while I was doing my own thing. The point is, one of the girls that we knew was having a birthday bash at a club in Manhattan. He told me that I should come because no one has seen me since I went to that school. I figured it would be fun, so I went and asked Kenniya to accompany me. Without discussing it, we ended up matching. She wore a red short sleeve shirt that drooped in the middle, exposing part of her stomach and revealing that she wasn't wearing a bra. She also wore red open toe heels and black tights. I wore a red button down, black jeans, black tennis shoes and a black fitted. Man, we sure did look good together. Upon arrival, I walked ahead of Kenniya, not to lead her in but to make it look like she wasn't with me. Yes, you guessed it, I was up to no good. We found Derek, his date and all who came to celebrate on the second floor of the club. We did the basic greetings and then I started conversing with one of the females I recognized in the group. She asked who was the girl that came with me and was she my "girl". That's when I remembered that I didn't even introduce her. I told her that her name was Kenniya and then quickly stated that she was not my "girl." I called Kenniya over to meet the group, well at least the ones I knew. Derek and I were the only two guys in that group of ten so we naturally paired off together. After scanning the club and talking about what females we saw, I noticed Kenniya standing off to the side by herself. I stared at her for a bit, just watching her body language. I watched her turn down a few guys' advances and seemed to start to get irritated. I then called the birthday girl, Derek and the ones that I knew to the bar to take shots at the bar. I also called Kenniya over but she declined for whatever reason. I'm guessing that she wasn't feeling the setting so instead she stood off to the side while the rest of us threw the shots back. We took a few more shots then joined the group who didn't partake. The night went on with Kenniya secluding herself from everybody else, so I had to make her as comfortable as possible all the while trying to mingle with the group. I can't say that I really was having fun, I was just socializing. No one really danced, most of the group remained in their seats and the place was pretty much empty for the size of the club. A couple more hours went by however, the energy in the room remained the same. Derek must have been thinking the same thing as I was because he told me that he was leaving and invited me to his house. He then added that Kenniya and I could spend the night if we wanted to. We said our goodbyes, gave out hugs then departed for his house. When we got to his car, I briefly looked over Derek because I wasn't sure of how much alcohol he consumed. He lived in downtown Brooklyn, in a condo, on the 23rd floor, with a view that was spectacular. The four of us talked for a little while then Derek started to set us up with a bed on the living room floor. He and his date retired to his room, while Kenniya and I prepared to lay down. It wasn't long before we heard moaning coming from Derek's room. We were jealous because Kenniya was on her period, so instead her and I just talked. She asked me if I was talking to other women and I said *"yeah"*. I could tell that she didn't like my response but she had no choice other than to respect it. She said with her eyebrows raised that she didn't want to be just another girl on my list. I frowned then, said *"who said that you even were on my list?"* Kenniya looked shocked and turned on at the same time. Next thing I knew we were on the topic of a relationship. Somehow, she convinced me to be with her. I think it was the mixture of alcohol and her looking at me with almond eyes, either way on March 26 at three something in the morning, we made it official. We finally went to sleep with thoughts of sex that we couldn't have, yet we were excited for what was to come. Later that morning, we all left so Derek could take everyone home. We dropped off his date first then along the way to drop Kenniya and I off, we decided to stop at a diner. We ordered breakfast and as we ate, I pulled Derek to the side to ask him what he thought of Kenniya. He said that she was pretty and that she seemed "cool". I nodded and told him the story of how we made it official at his place. I glanced over to where Kenniya was sitting and noticed she was getting impatient, so I ended the conversation there. After the bill was paid, we departed and headed for my house. On the way Kenniya suggested that we go back to her place. We got dropped off, then I packed some clothes and was off to her apt. We had to take the A train to 34th st then take a train to New Jersey which took over an hour. It was a good thing that she didn't live too far from the train because I was restless from the long ride. Kenniya lived in a 2-bedroom apartment, on the 2nd floor of a 3-story building. I remembered she told me that she had a 3-year-old daughter, so I asked where she was. She said that her daughter was at her grandmother's house for the weekend. When we got inside, Kenniya hospitality was on over time. She assisted me in taking some of my clothes off, went and got what I needed to take a shower and then took my dirty clothes to the washing machine that was conveniently downstairs. While I was washing up, she started to cook. Can anybody say "future wife". After I showered and put on a change of clothes, she led me to the living room and told me to watch T.V while she prepared dinner. Every now and again, Kenniya would come and massage my shoulders and ask if I needed anything. Now, I didn't know if it was genuine or if it was a show but whatever it was, it was working. After the food was ready, she brought me a drink and a plate which consisted of broccoli, rice and chicken. She warned me that the rice might be a little salty. I'm guessing that she was nervous because it was. Nevertheless, I still ate everything she made. When I was done, she took my plate then went to shower herself. That night I went to sleep with a smile on my face. It just couldn't get any better than this. Oh, so I thought...The next morning, I woke up to the smell of breakfast but when I tried to climb out of bed, Kenniya came from nowhere and stopped me. She instructed me to lay back down and wait for her to come back. I complied without hesitation, excited about what was to come. She returned shortly with a big plate of food. There were eggs, bacon, sausage, pancakes, biscuits, toast, orange juice and milk. Right then and there, I decided that I was going to marry her and that I needed to tell her my secret before this went any further.

Chapter 4

Unruly

I made a lot of bad decisions in my life. Although I knew better
somehow, I found myself doing something stupid or in trouble.
If it wasn't rolling tires down some stairs to hit passing cars or
shooting paintballs at shelter women, then I was trespassing on
someone's property or stealing drugs from my cousin. I know
you're reading this and thinking "what the hell?" Let me
explain...My cousin was a mini drug lord. I'm not sure of how
much of the east he controlled but I do know the "hood" I lived
in; he was boss. He had foot soldiers everywhere on my side of
town. What made it easier for my cousin and his team to "push"
drugs was the fact that my uncle worked at this grocery store
around the corner from my house. They basically used the store
as a stash spot. As soon as you walked in the store, there were a
few arcade games on the left. My friends and I used to go to
play faithfully and the guys would look after us. There was
Punisher, Street Fighter and Mortal Kombat. One day while I
was playing the arcade, one of the guys came in the store to
grab a brown paper bag from behind one of the arcade games,
he then left and returned once more to put the brown paper
back where he got it. I don't get why they were not more
discreet with what they were doing, especially in front of kids. I
guess they thought that we would never do anything stupid like
what I was about to do. My curiosity led me to wanting to know
what was in that brown paper bag still, I knew I could not just
simply ask. Instead, when no one was looking, I reached behind
that same arcade, took the brown paper bag and put it in my
hoody. I must have looked highly suspicious because as soon as
I walked out the store, I heard one of the guys yell "*a yo, come
here*". I immediately started running. I figured that I was being
chased so I panicked and ended up throwing the bag over the

fence, then ran to my house. I flew up my stairs, busted through the doors, while wondering the whole time, what was the contents in that brown paper bag. Well, I got what I wanted...I found out what it was but not in the way I would have liked. The guy who caught me came to my house and told my sisters what I've done. Then the next thing I knew, I was being held upside down by my sisters and beaten like a pinata. Then it happened...crack bottles and money fell like candy, all over the floor. My sisters were doing a number on me but I still was fascinated at how much money and drugs came out of my sweatshirt. Now that I'm older, I understand the severity of my actions. If it hadn't been for my blood tie, I could have been killed. There are some things you just don't do, point blank and period. It was like trouble found me or more like I found it. For instance, since my favorite color is red, I wore it as much as I could. To the point that by the time I got to high school, a few females were calling me "Red". The gangs that were around my neighborhood were mostly "Bloods", so it made it easier to wear. Around this time, people were getting cut, sliced and stabbed for wearing red like that but because I knew most of them, I was somewhat exempt. They would try to show me how to wear their "flag", teach me their codes, handshakes and blood oath; basically, they wanted me to join their gang. I didn't want to join yet I would still hang around them. I was oblivious to the fact that if the wrong person caught me, it would be a bad day for me. There was this time where I came close to that bad day. I had to be about 15yrs old, I think. I was wearing red like any other day and in addition, I had the red bandana with me. It hung boldly out the right side of my back pocket. I was walking from Howard projects (not my area) I believe, when a "Blood" who didn't know who I was, stopped me and asked, *"what that red be like?"* Now, in response, I am supposed to have a very crucial specific answer and if my answer is bogus or I don't know, the outcome can be less than pleasing to say the least. I told him that I wasn't "Blood" but I knew a lot of them as if that was a legitimate answer. I then told him what was taught to me.

He told me that I still needed to be careful because other fellow gang members don't take that too lightly. He walked off and I kept walking back to my "hood". I told my friends all that happened but not because I was shook up, just because I wanted to share my day. They said that I could have had my face cut open, amongst other things. That encounter didn't stop me from "flagging" or wearing red for that matter. Not only that, I started hanging around the "Bloods" that I knew even more. I even started beefing with whoever they were beefing with and fighting whoever they were fighting. I didn't even know what the reasons were behind the fights. I didn't ask and to be frank at the time, I didn't care. After a while I grew tired of "jumping" people, especially after getting arrested for it. I was walking to the "chicken spot" when I saw one of the "Bloods" I knew, he suddenly started jogging and telling me to follow. I was curious so I proceeded to follow him. We ran for a short while to find a bunch of other guys surrounding this one guy. Funny thing is, for as many guys there were, they all were hesitant. It wasn't like the kid was big or anything. All he had was a belt that he was swinging when someone got to close. The cat and mouse thing got boring, so I decided to attack the kid first. I landed a punch, my face barely missing his belt buckle, then everybody else took that opportunity to attack him too. Before any severe damage was done, sirens rang in the background. Everybody stopped in their tracks, looks were exchanged, then we all scattered like roaches. My silly self could have got away however, I basically handed myself over to the cops. I was one of two to get caught. I was blessed because they didn't charge me with anything gang related, and the kid didn't press charges. I stayed in the precinct for a few hours, then was released with a date to be at court. I was happy to be out of jail but the thought of being there made me pensive. I re-envisioned the whole experience. From the cold steel around my wrists to me being behind bars. The feeling of the eyes of the officers, like they were passing judgment and thinking I was just another black statistic. To be honest, they were right. I did not want to ever go through that again but unfortunately, I went through it a few more times. I got arrested for possession of marijuana, though I never sold weed a day in my life. A few years later, I was dating this girl named Yolanda and one night, I left her house to go to the store. After I got what I needed from the store, a random Caucasian man stopped me to ask for some weed. I told him that I did not have any but I know who does. I started to tell him where to go but decided that was a bad idea since they did not know him. I told him that I could get it for him, trying to be helpful, I guess. He handed me $10.00 and said that he would wait on the corner. I nodded, walked away and went to retrieve what was requested. At this point, you're wondering how come my alarms were not going off right? I knocked on the door, made the transaction then walked back to where he was waiting, handed him the bag of weed then turned to head back to Yolanda house. It was not long before I heard banging at her door. I peered out the window to see at least eight undercover cops standing outside of the door. My body said *"run"* though my mind asked, *"what would I be running from?"* Suddenly, I heard a loud bang, then another. Before I knew it, there were two doors broken and I was being pinned down by several cops. To add insult to injury, the whole time that I was down, someone was driving their knee repeatedly in my ribs. Yolanda was taken out of the shower and told to lay on the floor in her towel while several cops searched the house for drugs. Of course, they did not find anything and they must have felt stupid because they charged me with criminal mischief, possession and something else. On the paperwork, they said that It was me who had broken the doors in. They thought I was a dealer since I gave the undercover cop the bag of weed, be that as it may, I learned a hard lesson; that cops could play dirty. I had to go to court for a few months before they finally threw the case out. Lucky me...If only I knew how to stay my ass out of trouble. Too bad it was wishful thinking.

Chapter 5

What's done in the dark

Kenniya and I were still going strong. I went back to her house but this time she had her daughter with her. At the time Kenniya's daughter Solace was three. Solace looked like a darker version of her mother. She was very energetic, smart and talkative. It took no time at all for Solace to warm up to me. It could have been that she was just missing male attention. I pretty much entertained her the entire time. The day ended with me feeling content with how things were going, however that was when one of my skeletons started knocking at my closet door. Better yet, it called. It called at 2:00am while I laid next to Kenniya. I argued with my skeleton, telling it to leave me alone and to make matters worse, Kenniya was staring at me. She did not say anything, she just kept staring a hole in the side of head. When I got off the phone, I played it off like it was a crazed ex, that was still living in the past. I should have just come clean and told her my secret right at that moment. I was nervous, I mean, how do you tell someone you are with that you're engaged to another woman. Kenniya did not even question me, which made me feel even more guilty. The skeleton's name was Vanessa. On one hand, I felt bad for how I treated Vanessa though then again, I did not. I met her during A.I.T, which is Advanced Individual Training in the Army. We were both in the same unit. At the time, I was kind of dealing with somebody back home though, that relationship was pretty much over. Anyway, I did not notice my soon to be fiancé until one morning, she said something sarcastic to me. We were turning in linen and while waiting for my turn, I was conversing with a few of the guys that I knew since Basic Training. What started as a low murmur, ended in loud chatter. Then out of nowhere, I heard Vanessa say *"yall a bunch of individuals"*, followed by *"you can't train everybody*". I looked over my shoulder without bothering to turn all the way around and said in response "*don't act like your signature came out of patriotism*". One of the guys was whispering something about Vanessa and her friend being the best-looking females in our unit. I finally turned to see what they were talking about. Vanessa was Hispanic and Black. She was about 5'2, had long black, fair skinned and thick in all the right places. What really caught my attention were her eyes. They were hazel and very captivating. I had a feeling that she wanted me. My feelings were confirmed when I caught her staring at me while we were standing in formation. Later that day, I bumped into her at a recreational center. Our conversation was brief yet, we already knew that we wanted each other. The next day we sat next to each other during a briefing. She wrote me a note as if we were back in high school. We exchanged notes through the whole briefing. From then on, we were damn near inseparable. Keep in mind that during training, fraternizing was prohibited however, we were around each other so much that the Drill Sergeants did not even try to stop us. Although I found time to sleep with other females there, Vanessa was pretty much my "boo thang", so I tried to be as discreet as possible with what I did with other women. There was this one time I was suspected of creeping still, I always was one step ahead. I was downstairs after hours with a handful of other soldiers, including a platoon Sergeant. We all were smoking; some were smoking while music was blasting in the halls. In our building, none of the rooms had doors so I was able to peek into each room. I saw people dancing, two girls kissing and a couple having sex. One of the girls there would flirt with me whenever I was not with Vanessa. Her name was Lianna. She was about 5'5, her skin was a smooth chocolate and she had a big Alabama butt. For a while, Vanessa stayed around me until she had to use the bathroom. As soon as she left, I grabbed Lianna, took her to the room and immediately put lockers in front of the entrance. We had sex one time for about ten minutes. I wanted to go another round, however I knew any more time with her would be risky.

We both got dressed however, instead of leaving the way I came; I made my exit through the window. Since all the doors were locked, I had to climb the catwalk to get to my second- floor window. I came back downstairs and acted like nothing happened. When my roommate saw me, he ran up to me and said that Vanessa was looking for me and that she brought an entourage to help her find me. He continued by telling me all that transpired while I was gone. Apparently, Vanessa and her crew went upstairs to try to find me and when I was nowhere to be found, someone told her that I might be in the room with the lockers pushed in front. Upon hearing that, she went to the end of the hallway to locate the room with the lockers pushed in front to see who exactly was in there. She then shoved the lockers out her way to find Lianna laying on the bed and the window open. It was suspected that I could have been there. When my roommate was finished giving me the rundown, he asked if I was in there. I did not trust my roommate, so I told him no. At that moment, Vanessa and her friend walked up to me, inquiring of my whereabouts. I told them that I went upstairs for a moment to get something. She said that she was upstairs but she did not see me. I figured I was going to need supporting evidence, so I called out to this guy that I was cool with and asked him to confirm my story. He did exactly as I expected, backing my story and saving me from further questions. I laughed inwardly and thought of the Gingerbread man screaming *"catch me if you can"*. Vanessa and I made it to the end of training with no more mishaps. We ended up going our separate ways. She went to Kentucky and I went back to NY. I thought that would be the last I saw of her but she wrote me an email that was touching. It read

"The time we shared meant the world to me. You taught me a lot and I will cherish every moment of our time. If I never see you again, I want you to know that I care for you and if you ever need me, I'll be there".

I emailed her back saying

"Thank you and I enjoyed myself too".

She called a few days later seemingly distraught. She was upset because her unit was to deploy to Afghanistan in two months. We talked for a while, reminiscing about A.I.T and talking about how she missed me. She expressed that she was afraid to go to the Middle East during this time. I did not know what to say because how do you tell someone to not worry, when soldiers were coming home in body bags. She then started to joke about getting married and having a baby so she would not have to go. That is when the conversation became serious. She asked, *"why don't you and I get married and have a baby?"* I laughed, thinking she was playing. She asked again however, this time sounding more earnest. I asked if she was serious and she said *"yeah, why not?"* She added that she liked me a lot and that she would love to have a little boy that looked like me. I thought for a min, contemplating if I could go through with it. I thought of home and how getting away might not be a bad idea. I did not love her still, I thought that I would be fine with settling. Besides, I would be saving her from GOD knows what. I finally said, *"let's do it"*. After asking if I was serious, she screamed with joy. We planned for her to come to NY and then we took the necessary steps to get married in court. We filled out all the paperwork and registered to be married. We were going to do it as soon as she got her first break. Funny thing was that neither one of us looked excited. After that was done, we spent about a week in a half together before she left. The day Vanessa had to leave was emotional. I took her to JFK, arriving a few hours before her flight. The airport personnel let me come in the terminal to see her off since we were both in the military. When her flight was ready to depart, she burst into tears. I think she was crying out of fear, rather than for me. I hugged her for a minute before walking away. I walked to the elevator and got in. The doors closed, then reopened, when it did, I seen Julie standing there with eyes full of water. She could not stop crying. I immediately got out to console her. I am guessing that the staff watched her dash to get to me because they were all looking at us with sympathy. Some of the onlookers were even crying. I walked her back, gave her some encouraging words and then she turned to board the plane. All I could do was silently send my prayers. GOD speed.

Chapter 6

Birthday Madness

April 20, 2011

Kenniya's Letter to me

I honestly have no clue why I'm even writing this while I'm sitting in class. Obviously, I'm not paying this poor lady any attention. I feel like writing and as usual you crowd my thoughts. I can't really explain why but who can really, as to why you constantly think about a specific person. I don't mean to think about you but I could be talking about why the sky is blue and I'll throw you in the conversation. "Oh, my boyfriend has a nice pair of blue jeans." Got the person looking at me like "wait what?" lol (Don't judge me). My goal turns out to be, during the day, to consciously stop thinking about you. Think it'll work? Don't even answer that because knowing you, you probably got some cocky thought like "Hell no, I'm Shawn Harris" shut up! I guess since I'm always writing about you, I could at least tell you directly. I tell you verbally but whenever you want to ask some random questions about how I feel you can refer to this, ALTHOUGH you're going to make me answer anyway. I tend to constantly think about what this is going to be like me and you. My grandmother used to tell me all the time to take things as they come to you because you'll stress yourself out trying to prepare for the future but I can't help it, you make me nervous. Mainly because I don't know 100% of what to expect from you. Part of me feels like you'll make me a much stronger person in some areas but your forcefulness scares me. Who, it might be beneficial in the ways that you get me to do things I think to do but wouldn't be brave enough to do. (yeah, I flipped my paper upside down, so what).

I obviously like you a lot and I'm willing to try or else I wouldn't be here. For some odd reason, you have kind of like a gravitational pull (don't laugh at my analogy). Bottom line is I can't promise that we'll have a perfect relationship but if you promise to try, I promise that I'm staying. I can't promise that you won't make me mad and sometimes I'll cry but I promise to forgive you as long as you promise to say I'm sorry. I can give you my all with the return of yours as long as you take care of it, so that I may take care of yours. I didn't write this letter as an agreement or to show my expectations, it was just because you were on my mind and I wanted to tell you.

The relationship between Kenniya and I was only a month in before we had our first physical altercation. I had planned a birthday get-together for myself at BBQ's in Times Square. I invited about fifteen people or so. Family, friends and women that I had "history"with. Honestly, I don't even know why I invited any of the girls, especially Crystal. Crystal wanted me to be with her "bad" and I knew it. I guess I just wanted it to be about me and somewhat didn't care about how any of them felt regarding me and Kenniya. Selfish, I know. I took Kenniya with me but by the way I treated her, I was better off leaving her behind. When I got there, it was about four people, including Crystal who was already waiting for me. I greeted the few that were there and made it my business to speak to Crystal last. She went to hug me but I stopped her and shook her hand. The smile that was on her face, quickly vanished. Although Kenniya was not close by, I knew she was watching my interactions. Crystal asked, *"what was the matter?"* I said, *"I am here with somebody"* and then pointed to Kenniya. As if on cue, Kenniya walked over to where I was standing. She must of not like what she was seeing or the vibes because she asked Dominique and I *"why were we talking about her?"* with hostility in her voice. I calmly said *"relax, I was just telling her who I was here with".* I could tell Crystal was uncomfortable because she walked off. From then on, Kenniya made it her business to make it known that she and I were together. She would touch me every chance she got and would grab my shirt by the collar. I am not going to lie, I thought it was kind of cute. About thirty minutes later, everyone else arrived. We were then seated but since our group was so large, the staff had to put two tables together. Kenniya sat on my left and Crystal sat on my right, trying not to be obvious. I was nervous at first because I did not want Crystal flirting and most of all I did not want Kenniya to jump on her. I had to shake my head at myself because I was being messy. We all talked, we laughed, drank and everybody seemed to be enjoying themselves. So far so good. If I was not eating, I was socializing with everybody and taking their shots. When I sat back down, Crystal slipped me a card without Kenniya noticing. Right then, I should have told Crystal to cease and desist but I was too intoxicated to think logically. I did not want to open it, at the same time, I also did not want to be rude, so I quickly looked at it and put it down. I was not as slick as I thought because Kenniya was staring a hole through the side of head, though I never turned to meet her gaze. At this point, I was drunk and having fun still, Crystal was trying to indirectly ruin it. She kept finding reasons to talk to me or be around me. I tried to not engage in lengthy conversations with her so I would give her short responses and then walk away. The check came, we paid the bill and lingered outside. We decided to take a group picture, so we asked the cameraman who was nearby to take a photo of us. After the picture was taken, one of my friends came up to me and told me that Kenniya was livid. I was told while the picture was being taken, Kenniya was calling me to stand next to her nevertheless, I never heard her. To add insult to injury, Crystal managed to stand next to me right before the photo was taken. I was then shown the picture and sure enough there was Crystal with her arm around my waist. I shook my head. I needed to find Kenniya because I knew she was perturbed. As I was looking for her, Crystal walked up and inquired about the card that she gave me. I told her I did not know, with that she turned to head back upstairs to find it. Just then, I spotted Kenniya glaring at me a few feet away. I approached her with every intent of apologizing, be that as it may, she jumped down my throat before I could open my mouth. She was shouting and putting her hands in my face which I tried to let her get out. Even so, I was losing my patience, especially because I was drunk. I grabbed her arms and started yelling back, trying to excuse my behavior. Of course, our commotion created a crowd and in turn grew the attention of the police. After all it is, 42nd st. My homeboy pulled me across the street before the cops got there and to keep me from getting arrested. He told me to leave but I did not want to abandon Kenniya so I made it my business to find her. As I was heading across the street, here comes Crystal with the card again, telling me that Kenniya threw it in the garbage. I shrugged then walked past her to continue my search. I found Kenniya fuming by the train station, looking like she was ready to strangle somebody. She did not say much to me and I did not know what to say except that I was sorry. She was quiet the whole train ride but I kept apologizing and kissing her face anyway. We stayed at a hotel that night and in the morning, we departed to head to Kenniya's place. We had a better day than we had yesterday and later that same night, she gave me my birthday gift. She handed me a card with a poem written in it. Not only that Kenniya had purchased a pink stripper pole and had it set up in the living room. She had on this black lace one piece and black heels. There was also chocolate and strawberries at my leisure. Something sweet for something sweet. Boy, was I turned on. She lit some candles, turned some music on and started to dance for me. I couldn't take my eyes off of her. She worked the pole, gave me a lap dance and fed me chocolate off her finger. After her performance, I wanted to take pictures of her, so I told her to put on my uniform. Man, this woman was a feast for the eyes. I took some photos and added handcuffs to the mix for some kinkiness. When I snapped enough pictures, she sat me down, took off my clothes, put the handcuffs on me and started giving me head. She slowly sucked on it, while trying to fit as much of it in her mouth as she could. It was mind blowing, I put my head back and groaned under my breath. She continued to give me head until she knew that I was close to cumming, then she rose from her knees and said not yet. Next, Kenniya straddled me, grabbed my rock-hard dick and slid down on it. She started to ride me, going up and down ever so seductively. She softly said, *"daddy don't cum until I tell you to"*. Every time that she knew that I was about to cum, she would stop, driving me crazy. She kissed me while riding me and when she felt my leg quiver, she got off. I chuckled and asked *"baby, why are torturing me?"* She smiled in return and said, *"we have not even started yet"*. We started to kiss though, she stopped so she could turn around. She rode me backwards, looking back occasionally to show me that she was not here to play. It did not take long for us both to come close to the brink of exploding. Her body trembled and her pussy walls started to contract, I then quickly pushed my pelvis up as far as I could letting all of me flow inside all of her. We both let out a big sigh, high off pure ecstasy. This was one for the books. The following day, Kenniya made us breakfast. She knew that I loved to eat because she always gave me big plates of food. There was never a time where I did not finish her food. The best dish she ever made was steak, corn and shrimp over rice. It was so delicious. Her talents did not stop there though. This girl could sing, dance, write poetry/songs and draw. Kenniya was also good at doing hair and make-up. She was the woman of my dreams so I could not understand why I was unfair to her. She had all these great qualities about her and I could not give her what she deserved. Men can be so stupid. Mind you, I am a mama's boy. I love my mother to death. The point is, I would not want anyone to hurt my mother so why would I hurt all these girls, least of all Kenniya. I had to figure out my issues and get rid of them. One of them being a short fuse. I could not stand being stepped on or bumped so when it happened by accident or not I would either say something or hit them back. Even as a kid, I had anger issues. I got mad at this lady for being upset at the fact that I was making fun of her. She was so bothered that she threatened to get her sons on me and because I was immature, I threw a football at her and yelled *"go get them"*. In elementary, I threatened my 6th grade teacher with a machine gun that I did not have. I also fought my substitute teacher in 5th grade because I did not like the way he threw me out of the room. I know I was disrupting the class still, he did not have to grab me up like that. He scratched me in the process, so I felt that I was justified. In the 7th grade this kid kept talking about me while we were in class so as soon as the bell rang and we were in the hallway, I beat him up. The stories just get worse and worse. No, another beating was not going to make me get my act together. Refer to chapter 2. I needed love, affection and attention. Not just from my mom but from my dad as well. That is exactly where it all came from and it was not until I met Kenniya that I figured it out. She got the worst of it. Trey Songz said it right "hard to believe that I treated someone beautiful, so ugly".

Chapter 7

When I was a boy, I thought like a boy

1 Corinthians 13:11

Kenniya continued to impress me and the more she did, the worse I felt about not telling her the truth. There was this one time where I almost told her my secret however, I chickened out. It was like I had a lump in my throat that I could not get out. I did not want to scare her away. I really liked her and did not want to lose her. So, I chose not to tell her, at least not now. I went to her apartment after work where Kenniya was already waiting for me. When I walked in the door, she told me to close my eyes and then proceeded to blindfold me. She led me to a chair that she had placed in the middle of the living room. When she took it off, I was beyond excited. The living room was lit with candles, she had edibles set up on my left and wine set up on my right. She stood in front of me wearing a red lace negligee. Damn this woman is pulling out all the stops. She fed me a few edibles and gave me a sip of wine. She then handed me a small piece of folded paper. I opened it and it said

> *"This is the beginning of a new start; I want you to have all of me so I'm giving you my heart. Let's play a game...I hid my heart, and you must follow the clues to find it. First clue: "You put me on when you're cold".*

I shook my head and smiled. The first one was easy. It could not have been anywhere else, other than my coat. Sure enough, it was in my pocket. It was another folded piece of paper and it read

> *"I am here, you have found me. You are looking for the next but hmmm, where could I be? I'm tucked away in what seems like a box all day. She only pulls me out when she wants to play or*

to be sexy".

It took me a second because I was high but it was not long

before I figured out the next clue was in her lingerie draw. *Good job! You seem to be doing well. If you don't get this one, you'll always have to ring a bell. I am under a storage space; I'm paid no mind. Underneath a loud thing, I might be hard to find".*

I found the next one under the entertainment system.

I thought that would be hard for you. Not stumped yet, you know what to do. In this I get heated, I have a countdown, even though you have the oven, I still feel needed'.

I quickly walked to the microwave and found the next note inside.

"Ok, I am one of the last...You and the love of your life have

slept on me in time past. She has to lay on top, don't move too far or else you will both flop".

I ran to her bed with confidence yet, nothing was there. Damn edibles lol. I had to read the note several times before it dawned on me that the next clue was in the couch. The last note said,

"you found me but one more clue, I'm where her heart should be".

I looked at her confusedly. She asked, *"where should my heart be?"* With the biggest grin, she added *"it's not metaphorical".* I looked at her chest, walked over and put my hand over the top of her negligee to find a key. When I went to remove the key, she grabbed my hand, looked me dead in the eyes and said, *"I love you".* I smiled and kissed her. She then led me to the bedroom. I watched her slowly climb on top and slowly crawl to the middle before turning on her back. She then gave me the "come here" gesture with her index finger, while giving me a mischievous smirk. I walked to the edge of the bed taking hold of one of her feet. I kissed the top of her foot, easing my way down her shin, up her thighs until I got to her lower pelvis. I then did the same thing to her other leg kissing every inch. By the time I got to her pelvis she was jerking her hips left, right, up and down. I reached down and felt her juices between her enclosed lips. I lowered myself to part them with my tongue. I then spread her legs wide open to get a full view of my meal. At first I started slow by kissing her inner thighs, giving her light kisses of the opening of her vagina and softly licking her outer lips. The way her body shivered made my dick jump. I started to feel animalistic. I wrapped my arms around her legs and lifted her pelvis off the bed so I could taste her at an angle. I sucked on her lips, stuck my tongue inside, making sure my lips were just as much involved. I put her down then started to tease her with my rock-hard dick, only allowing the head of me to enter her. I did that for a few seconds until I felt that I tortured her enough. Then I pushed in the rest, easing myself into the curvature of her pussy. I could barely keep my composure because of how good she felt. I sexed her crazy for a while then I whispered in her ear *"I want you to take over"*. I rose up so that we could switch positions. Kenniya straddled me with her slender legs. She moved up and down on my erected member to a slow beat that only she could hear. She bit her bottom lip and then started to make small circles with her hips. Without thinking we interlocked our hands as she rode me rhythmically. To keep from cumming, I had to stop her and get up and change our positions again. This time, I put her on all fours, allowing a full view of her tattoos. She had one paw print on each cheek that made her ass look even more irresistible. I grabbed her waist, then I shoved my dick in but I stopped so she could adjust so she could comfortably take all of me. When she was ready, I started to make short thrusts. My thrusts got longer and my pace got faster. I pushed down on her back so that her ass was higher in the air. By this point, I was at my peak, so I bit myself a little to keep from ejaculating. It didn't help that her moans were ever so sexy. I motioned her to lay flat on her stomach. When she did, I layed on top and grinded her hard. I kissed the nape of her neck, her back, her shoulders and finally I turned her face to kiss her. Right then I lost it. I did one final thrust while releasing everything I held back inside of her. All I could think was "man this woman is something else". As amazing of a woman as I thought that she was, I still struggled with fully opening up to her. It has been two months and she has already said "I love you" several times without me saying it back. Truth be told, Kenniya scared me. I knew she would be capable of removing my shell and I wasn't ready to be exposed. I didn't want to be that guy who falls madly in love with a woman and I get hurt. I seen and heard about women doing that all the time. Leaving men for their brothers or taking the kids while he's away. On top of that I've been with so many women who were with someone else. Women who were in relationships, engaged and who had families.

Years Ago...

There was a time where I was eating out a woman while she was on the phone with her man and her kids were in the next room. Every time she went to moan, she muted her phone. Grimy right? I guess we both were. There was another time that I knew the guy personally and still slept with his kid's mother. I even had a guy walk into his apartment while I was laid up with his child's mother. He didn't even react; he just walked straight to the back and never came back out. I could keep going but the point is...if those were conniving women, what made mine so different. Why can't it happen to me? What makes me so special? What's ironic, I watched my dad do it to my mom. Yes, I could have vowed to be different, still sometimes stuff like that can have a negative psychological effect on a kid. Then there were family who I've watched manipulate men. I listened to how they would talk about them. So, I told myself that I would never fall for a girl. As a result, I played around with countless hearts. Women flocked to me and I toyed with every one of them. I was good at it too. I used to walk ahead of girls, just to talk to my friends, disregarding that they were there with me. I left another outside with my friends while I went into someone else's apartment to have sex. Those were my teenage years, it got worse as I got older. I had two girls go with me to see the ball drop, which surprised me because they never questioned who the other was. I invited different girls I was dating to my birthday events and worst of all, I brought women to other women's houses when they weren't home. I had no regard for their feelings. I knew that when I had a girl in high school write me a suicide note and all I did was show my friends like it was funny. Thank GOD she never went through with it. A few years later another overdosed-on pills and had her stomach pumped. Although, asking me to see her in the hospital I refused. Now that I'm in a different mindset, I feel horrible for all I've done. I even tried to make amends with a few of them. Especially my former female best friend named

Rosa. She was a pretty Latin girl from Ecuador. She had long jet-black hair, almond milk skin, about 5'6 with wide hips. What really gave Rosa her appeal was her long eyelashes. I met Rosa in freshman year in High School. At first, we didn't like each other, however, as time went on, we eventually became friends. For ten years we remained that way. I met her family and she met mine. We slept in the same bed together, smoked together, got drunk together and told each other our deepest secrets. Her family and mine wanted us to be together however, we on the other hand, did not agree. I loved Rosa and valued our friendship. I could tell her anything and everything without being judged. She knew more about me than the people who I grew up with. Regardless of how much time we spent together, never did I look at Rosa in a romantic way. I never even played with the idea. Then one day I did. Maybe it was everybody telling me that "we would make a great couple" that made me consider it. Maybe it was because I thought we could have the best of both worlds. Lovers and friends. We get along and the conversations are great, what can go wrong? Right? All I know is that, while we were texting about what "everybody" says about us, I said "let's try it". Rosa called me immediately to ask me if I was serious and if I was sober. I told her I was and in response she said, *"prove it"*. I asked her *"how so?"* She then told me to meet her in Manhattan at the bar she was at so that we could talk in person over drinks. I said *"ok"*, got ready and left to meet her. When I got there Rosa was already three drinks in. She told me that she had a Jager bomb and told me that I should try it. She ordered me three drinks so I could "catch up". I had to laugh to myself because I thought "this is what men do to women". We left the bar shortly after, walking and talking about her hidden feelings. I never knew that she even thought of me like that. Rosa never gave any indication, no clue, no crumb or anything for that matter to let me know that she was interested in me. I ended up kissing her, right then and there in the middle of the sidewalk. People walked around us while we just acted like they didn't even exist. After we finished locking lips, she asked me to get a hotel. I studied her for a bit and then said, *"not like this"*. As much as I wanted her, I didn't want our first time to be influenced by alcohol. Rosa kissed me again and said, *"I understand completely"*. I signaled for a cab, so she did not have to take the train while she was intoxicated. I held her hand as she got in and told her to text me as soon as she got in. The next time we got together, we definitely ended up at a hotel. I invaded her insides trying to prove to her that I was as freaky as I said I was. Allowing her to sit on my face and smother me with her wide hips and thick thighs. My tongue would wiggle in, out and around her pussy. She could never get enough of watching the way that her juices would gloss my face up. Rosa and I didn't stop at the hotel. We had sex on the stairs in a building, sex at my job, sex in a bathroom at a fastfood restaurant. We were inseparable for a few months until I met Kenniya. What I did next was blatant, insensitive and disrespectful. I bought Kenniya with me around Rosa's job to shop, only thinking about the high in retail that she worked next to on 5th ave in Manhattan. One of Rosa's coworkers saw me with Kenniya and told Rosa. When she questioned me about it, I was honest and told her everything, thinking I was doing the right thing. That was the beginning of the end for us. I guess I thought I could just stop playing the field, go cold turkey if you will. Truthfully, I didn't really know what I was even doing. I should have never even stepped to her knowing that I wasn't ready. After finding out about Kenniya we were still trying to work through it and still having sex. Nevertheless, I could tell that It was not the same between us. We never really discussed what happened and eventually just stopped talking all together. I was too busy in my own self absorbed world. I lost a friend because of my poor choices. She trusted me and felt that I could do no wrong, so it hurt her more being that I was her best friend. I just hope one day, she can forgive me. Damn...I am a true disappointment.

Chapter 8

Truth is the only safe ground to stand on

Summer was approaching and the relationship started to get crazy. At first, things were going smoothly. I finally told Kenniya that I love her. We were having fun and just enjoying each other's company. If we weren't wrestling or playing cards, we were outside in the rain, chasing each other through puddles. Then here we go back to arguing, back to me ignoring her and back to me sleeping on the couch. I knew Kenniya was very emotional however, since I didn't have patience, I had no idea how to deal with her. It didn't help that I didn't have relationship etiquette. I could not even keep up with any agreements that we had. For instance, whenever I went to NY, Kenniya wanted me to text or call every two hours. I did for a while, yet I stopped keeping track of time. It got worse when Vanessa came back to town. She was on a two week leave. Of course, most of that time was spent with me. It was cool because she was splurging on me. She took me out to eat, took me shopping, put cash in my pocket and paid a couple of my bills. I was so caught up in what I was doing, I would forget to text Kenniya entirely, making it seem like I was working a lot. I would make up a lie saying that I was drinking with my friends. I had to remember to at least text Kenniya whenever Vanessa was not around. The funny thing was Vanessa was creeping too. While we were walking getting ready to get something to eat, a guy called her. His name looked familiar. It did not take me long before I recognized his name in one of her comments on her Facebook post. Not only that but that was also the same name that sent a message to her inbox. All that was sent was *"hey"* then she deleted the message. Before she could pick it up, I grabbed her phone and answered. As soon as I did, he hung up. With a scowl on my face, I looked at Vanessa and asked her who he was and why he hung up. She said that he was her cousin and that he must have been nervous. From that day on, I started looking at her differently. Who am I to talk right? Still, I did not like the idea of being played. I saw his name again three days later, apparently, he was trying to reach her. I was more than suspicious; I was certain he was somebody she was dealing with just the same, I needed to know for sure. My opportunity came when he called while we were checking into a hotel. When I saw him calling, I took her phone and answered it. I said, *"Hello cousin"*. He took a pause then responded, *"can I speak to Vanessa?"* I said, *"sure but before you do, I wanted to introduce myself"*. *"I'm her fiancé and I would like to know if you are her cousin?"* I heard him sigh and then he said, *"ask her"* and then he hung up. I attempted to call back but it went straight to voicemail. At that moment, I no longer felt bad for what I was doing to her. I needed no explanation, when she tried, I cut her off and said that I needed time to process all that had happened. I pretended to be mad so I could get away to see Kenniya. I asked Vanessa to drop me off at my "friend's" house; however, since she was tired, she wanted me to drive instead. I drove to Jersey, which took me three and a half hours because I kept taking the wrong turn. I followed the GPS the best I could, even so, I must have been just as sleepy. When we finally made it to Kenniya house, I tried to be slick by parking a few yards down from the actual building that she lived in. Kenniya managed to peer her head out the window at the right time to see me getting out of the car. Apparently, she had been frequently looking out the window, waiting for me. I was glad that I was giving Vanessa the cold shoulder, otherwise I would have hugged her or something before departing. As soon as I walked in, she asked who the girl was. I lied and said that it was just a friend that I met at my unit. I quickly added that she had nothing to worry about. She then asked, "what took me so long?" The more I explained, the more it sounded like I was lying. She kept saying that my story sounded funny and kept saying, *"but hours though?"* After some "sweet nothings" and caresses of the skin, she finally dropped the subject. I stayed for a few days, being very attentive so that she wouldn't bring up the "girl" again. Kenniya must was meant to find out about Vanessa because she texted me while I was showing Kenniya something on my phone, which made her question me all over again. The text read *"Hey are you going to see me so we could talk about this?"* Kenniya took the liberty to respond for me, saying that I wasn't coming and that I was with someone. Then without a word, she gave me the phone back and walked out the door to get her hands and feet done. It could not have been no longer than five minutes after Kenniya stepped out the door that Vanessa called. I waited until the coast was clear before I called back.

Shawn: Hey

Vanessa: Babe who the hell was texting me?

Shawn: That is somebody that I started seeing recently.

Vanessa: Why? Why would you do that? I'm your fiancé.

Shawn: My fiancé is sneaky and can't be trusted. Who also been fucking her so-called "cousin".

Vanessa: That is my cousin.

Shawn: You're really trying it. Ok. Let's make it make sense. You tried to delete his message from Facebook, then he called several times but when I answered, he hung up. The funny thing is, when I asked him if he was your cousin, he could have just lied and said yes. He is not even a smart "side dude" but since he is a rookie, he blew up your spot by hanging up. "Cousins" don't do that. So, you tell me, who is he really?

Vanessa:......He is my ex.

Shawn: Now, we are getting somewhere.

I smiled internally because I was glad that she was messing with somebody else. It was going to make it easier to cut ties with her.

Shawn: How long have you been messing with your ex?

Vanessa: We have not been messing around, we have only been talking and I have not even seen him for a couple of years now.

Shawn: Well, you better go see him now because I no longer want to get married.

Vanessa fought against it and in spite of that, I would not budge. When I saw that she wasn't getting the message, I decided to take a different approach. I said, *"why would you want someone who doesn't want you?"* She was silent for a while but she finally said that if I wanted to end things, that I was going to regret it, then she hung up. I thought that she would go peacefully. I thought my decision would make us both happy, however she was angry. My sister said that Vanessa called her and threatened to have me thrown in jail and kicked out of the military. She said that Vanessa even came over to the house to speak to my mother about the whole situation. When she saw that contacting my family wasn't working, she started sending me explicit videos. I clicked on one and I was about to delete it still, my curiosity got the best of me and I opened the file. I don't know what possessed me to open it, especially because Kenniya was right in the next room when I did. I had only watched about ten seconds of the video when I heard her call my name and started walking to the room that was in. I closed it out as fast as I could. Nevertheless, I was not quick enough. She asked what it was that I just closed out. I told her that one of my friends sent me a stupid video. Instead of deleting the evidence, I kept it thinking she would just leave it alone. The dumb thing is, I knew better. I know when it comes to women and their suspicions, they're not leaving anything alone. They might be quiet about it but at the same time know that they are waiting for the right moment to get their answers. That is exactly what Kenniya did. She waited until I fell asleep, checked my emails and then the next thing I knew, I was awakened to a familiar sound. She had the laptop next to me, playing that same video on repeat and on maximum level. She was surprisingly calm still, she made sure that she expressed how disgusted she was.

Then she bombarded me with a bunch of questions. All I had to do was tell her the truth, I didn't even have a real excuse not to, except that she would have been mad. I stuck with the fact that my friend wanted me to see the video. She seemingly brought my lie though I didn't hear the end of it until I left for Kentucky a few days later. I wanted to talk to Vanessa in person about "us" and ending on a good note. I also wanted to tell her why so she can have the closure that she needed to move on. After explaining my reasons for wanting it to be over, she agreed that it was for the best. My main priority was making sure she wasn't carrying my baby. To my relief, she was not. I stayed with her for about a week, taking a tour of the cities. I even went to Tennessee since where she stayed was close to the border. Kenniya didn't suspect anything, so she didn't call me unless I called her because I told her that I was away on "orders". When I got back, things between us were going well again. We were having water fights in the house, playing with nerf guns and had movie nights with the kids. Even when Kenniya's mother complicated things, the fun we were having didn't waver. Then I was hit with unexpected news. One day in the midst of playing cards, Kenniya announced that she was pregnant. At first, I could not understand how because she was on birth control and yes, she was taking them. At least that is what I thought. I stopped questioning after a while. Part of me wanted a baby, the other part, not so much so when she asked how I felt, I told her that I'll support whatever decision she made. I think what happened next happened while she was pregnant because she would have killed me if she wasn't. All this time I kept the documents of my engagement hidden in her house and I wanted to get rid of them because they were haunting me. Although they were put away, just knowing they were there was bothering me. I decided to throw them out so while Kenniya was out, I took them from where they were and put them face down in the garbage. I didn't want to be found out so I don't know why I settled for the trash, I could have easily burned them or thrown them in the trash outside. Also, I knew that Kenniya was a bloodhound, so it was only a matter of time before she discovered them. I think my conscience had enough. Sure enough, something told her to look through the papers that she saw lying face down in the garbage. I remember I walked into the house from work and I was headed to the bedroom to greet her when I saw papers spread out across the bed with Kenniya at the end of it crying. When I got closer, my heart dropped, my face was pale and I just froze. I didn't know what to say. I mean, what could I say. She stopped sobbing long enough to ask, *"why didn't you tell me?"* I took a deep breath, let out a deep sigh and said, "I didn't know how". She continued to cry so I sat next to her with my head down, not saying anything for a few minutes. I then explained how I always wanted to tell her still, I could not find the right words. As I was speaking, Kenniya sobs suddenly stopped as if something just dawned on her. She asked me a fury of questions, piecing together the truth as I answered each one. The more the truth came out, the angrier she got. I tried to apologize to her, however Kenniya wasn't having it. She kept me at arms distance for the rest of the day. To be honest, I think if she had not been pregnant, she would have walked away. When we laid down that night, I kissed her softly until she allowed me to hold her. The next day, she woke up at 6am waving those same documents in my face, saying that the only way that she will forgive me is if we move. I immediately started my search for a new house. It took me a month and a half to find us a place. It was a 2-bedroom, 1 and a half bath house which wasn't too far from the apartment that we lived in. We both loved it because the house had a dining room in addition to the living room, a private backyard and a basement. The basement also came with the convenience of a washer and dryer. The only thing we didn't like was the location of the shower. The only way to get to it was through the master bedroom, which means that the kids would have to disturb us whenever they had to shower. It didn't take us long to move in since we left the furniture behind. We ordered all new furniture. A few days later the furniture started to come around 8am. Kenniya directed the movers on where she wanted everything. She was so excited. I was happy that she was happy. Some of the stuff that she ordered needed to be adjusted or put together. I had to go to work, so I told Kenniya to wait until I got off. She was so stoked that she had everything done by the time I got home. She put together both beds, the furniture was set up how she wanted it, dishes, supplies, clothes and everything else was all put away. A huge smile crossed my face and all I could think was "a woman will turn a house into a home". She walked up to me with a glass of wine, wearing a sexy satin red ball gown and said, *"this is a new start for the both of us, let's leave the drama behind"*.......... If only.

Chapter 9

Bad Blood

Kenniya's family did not like me. It didn't really matter because I wasn't too fond of them either. Kenniya did her best to keep her personal life away from her family. They didn't know much of what she did or who she dated. Kenniya told me stories about them that left a bad taste in my mouth before I even met them. She told me that they were nosy and that they would gossip about her. She also explained in detail how her mother was a tyrant who tried to dictate her parenting and her relationships. She explained how her step-dad was a molester who touched her when she was younger and how her sister was two-faced. They lived in Toms River about an hour away from her apartment and according to Kenniya, they never visited her. That quickly changed. Kenniya and I was about two months into our relationship when her step-dad "just so happened to be her neighborhood." He called her and said that he was in the area and wanted to stop by. Kenniya went to greet him downstairs to avoid him coming in but after a short while, she returned with her step-dad behind her. Apparently, he had to use the bathroom. When he saw me sitting on the couch in the living room, he stopped in the doorway and looked at Kenniya. She must have understood the look because she awkwardly said *"oh that's my boyfriend Shawn"*. I said *"hello"* however, he never responded. He just turned to her and said his goodbyes then he left. Looking confused, I asked Kenniya what was that all about. She said he asked to use the bathroom and she reluctantly led him up. She added that she feels like he just wanted to be nosy. She speculated that her daughter Solace must have mentioned me during one of her visits over there and he came to investigate. Knowing that he was going to tell her mother, she said it was only a matter of time before she received a phone call. They did her one better. About a week later, her mother and her sister decided to pop up unexpectedly. The day that they came Kenniya, her daughter and I was headed out so we all were in the middle of getting ready. Without any notice or a head's up, Kenniya mother and sister were calling her to say that they was down stairs. I was still in the shower so I told Kenniya to let me finish before she let them in. I quickly got out the shower and went into the bedroom to get dressed. Kenniya then told them that they could come upstairs and as soon as Kenniya opened the door, they started to complain. They were both upset that they had to wait downstairs for a while. What I couldn't understand was how could they be mad when they both showed up unannounced. Not to mention, the only reason they came over, was to be in her business. I was almost done getting dressed when I heard a knock at the bedroom door. It was Kenniya's mother telling me to hurry up. I was instantly annoyed. I came out expressionless trying my best not to show how I was actually feeling. She studied me for a bit before introducing herself. I thought to myself that she looked nothing like her daughter, except the lips. She was a medium brown, heavy set with dark brown eyes. She was assertive and made her presence known. She said *"Hi I'm Kenniya's mother Mrs. Johnson and who might you be?"* I reached out to shake her hand and said *"hey, I'm Shawn"*. I looked around for Kenniya but she was in her daughter's bedroom arguing with her sister about their wait time so I just pulled up a chair to the couch that Mrs. Johnson was on and sat down. Again, she spoke first. She asked *"do you live here?"* I said *"yes"*. She then asked *"so are you the man of the house?"* I said *"yes"*. Kenniya walked in leaving her sister behind to play with Solace just as Mrs. Johnson was asking her next question. She asked *"don't you think that it's too soon for you to be around Solace like that?"* Mrs. Johnson focused her eyes back on me and I quickly looked at Kenniya to see if she was going to reply nonetheless, since I did not see any indication of her responding I went ahead and answered her. I said *"maybe it was rushed and maybe it wasn't thought through, still whatever the case*

I'm here now". I then leaned in and with an arrogance I was unaware of at the moment and added *"I don't know what the future holds, be that as it may I do know whether now or later, what is meant to be, will be. What I do know is that I care for both your daughter and your granddaughter".* I looked over at Kenniya and noticed a slight smirk on her face. I diverted my eyes back at Mrs. Johnson who didn't seem amused at all. She darted her eyes to Kenniya then back at me and said *"How come you didn't meet us yet?"* I turned towards Kenniya signaling for her to answer this one. She caught on but she paused for a second knowing that her words would upset her mother. She then spoke softly, saying that she was not ready for any of them to meet me. Kenniya's mother's face scowled almost instantly. She asked *"why not?",* while glaring at Kenniya. Kenniya said *"because you like to interrogate".* That was exactly how I was feeling at the moment, as if I was under investigation. Mrs. Johnson shifted her attention to me, seemingly waiting for me to answer for her. When I didn't get the hint, she asked me flat out *"how come I didn't tell her to allow me, to meet the family?"* I said that I had left that up to Kenniya and I respected her decision. From there things went further downhill. It was apparent that Mrs. Johnson didn't like how the conversation was going because she started getting boisterous. I guess she thought if she spoke louder, that maybe I would break character. I ended our conversation by telling her that she was not going to intimidate me, then I walked away. I knew that Kenniya's mother and I would always be at odds. Time proved it to be so. Whenever there was a holiday or event Mrs. Johnson would invite Kenniya, Kenniya would ask her if I could come as well however, Mrs. Johnson would say no. Kenniya would then say *"well if he cannot come then I am not coming neither".* I would tell Kenniya that she should go anyway. I would argue the fact that they were still her family and her response would always be the same. She would say that they needed to respect my place in her life. No matter how much I tried to persuade Kenniya, she remained firm in her decision. Stubbornness was definitely a family trait. I understood where Kenniya was coming from, I just didn't want to come in between her and her family; even if they were not our favorite people at the time. I made the situation worse by letting an inappropriate picture of Solace on Facebook. No, nothing perverted, despite that I will admit that it was very immature. There was this one time Solace and I was in Kenniya's apartment while she was in school. Solace must have had a stomach virus because she had diarrhea. Instead of cleaning her up, I decided to tease her and take a picture of it. I sent it to Kenniya and since she thought it was funny, she posted it on her page. About a month later, Kenniya's mother called when she heard about the picture. She scolded and lectured Kenniya, telling her that it was wrong and embarrassing to Solace. Kenniya started to get frustrated so I took the phone from her to clear things up, especially because I felt solely responsible. I said *"hello, this is Shawn. Kenniya didn't put that picture up, I did".* Mrs. Johnson spoke harshly, *"who told you to get on the phone?"* Kenniya and I exchanged looks before I spoke again. I said *"I figured it was the right thing to do. It's not fair to Kenniya that she has to take blame for something I did".* I heard another voice speak this time. Apparently, Kenniya's step father was on the other line listening the whole time. He said calmly *"would you have did that to your own kid?"* I said *"yes".* He started to speak again but Mrs. Johnson interjected. "Well, we know who runs the house", I said to myself. She said *"that's why we don't like you".* The animosity in her voice was spewing through the phone. I ignored her remark and directed my attention to Kenniya's step father. I said *"William right?"* Mrs. Johnson interjected again by saying that his name was Mr. Johnson. I had to wonder, where was this man's balls? I said *"well I am Mr. Harris."* I continued *"I didn't find her sickness funny, however I did find some humor in the situation. Nevertheless it was taken down and never will it happen again".* Mrs. Johnson still was not pleased. She said *"Solace is not yours, when you have your own with my daughter, maybe then you can do what you want".* What she didn't know was Kenniya was currently carrying my child. Mr. Johnson asked me when could the four of us have a sit down and after quick consideration I said *"never"*. I felt like he let his wife seal our fate. He failed to at least tell his wife to calm down or take control of the situation. So I didn't feel like there was anything else for us to talk about. Mr. Johnson said *"Ok, then. Can you put Kenniya back on the phone"*. When Kenniya got back on the phone, Mrs. Johnson was speaking yet again, telling her that for now on they were going to talk to each other at least once a week to strengthen their relationship. They ended the conversation with that. After hanging up I wondered how long the phone calls would last. Nonetheless, what I was really looking forward to was telling Mrs. Johnson that she could not come to my house. See, we were moving soon and I wanted to give her the same courtesy as she gave me when it came to her house. Resentfulness is corrosive and we all find out, one way or another.

Chapter 10

Old habits die hard

You would think that the new move and the baby on the way would be enough to give us a "happy streak" but sadly things got worse. Don't get me wrong, I loved Kenniya, better yet I was in-love with her however, like a lot of men, I had a neural disease called "fuck boy". For some reason we have a tendency to fuck up a good thing as well as try to fix it when its already too late. The only thing I gave myself credit for, is not being sloppy with my infidelity. I'm not saying that it's something to be proud of. Fact of the matter was I was still a dog still, at least I wasn't blatantly putting it in her face. When we first got to the house things were ok. It's always ok in the beginning. We bathed together, played and prayed together. We had water fights around the house, we had our picnics on the living room floor and dinner dates inside. Then things went left and before I knew it, I was back to my trifling ways. I would go to New York every chance I got, making up any excuse to run to the big apple. Kenniya would complain about my absence and I would tell her that she was being too emotional. She figured buying me a game system would keep me home more. Which did work for a little while yet, when she saw that I was paying more attention to the game, she would stand in front the T.V half naked or she would turn the T.V off completely. I was neglectful, not just to her but also to the kids as well. She tried to get me to see that, however her efforts of making me more involved with the family was always met by stubbornness and pride. I had a brief moment of clarity, where I noticed that I was making her cry too often and in turn made me think that it was probably having a negative effect on my unborn child. I decided I needed to turn things around for the sake of my family and baby on the way. I started by implementing "family night" into our routine. I would read to Solace and my baby on the way. I purchased nerf guns and when it would rain, I'd take them out to play in it. I was on a roll, then I found myself doing everything she asked me not to do and then some. Knowing that she was insecure, I still would be on the phone with other women who I called "friends" for long periods of time. I would claim that I didn't have any past or current sexual encounters with them, which was a bold face lie. As expected, my relationship with them made her feel uncomfortable. To add to her discomfort, she caught me looking at some random female that I crossed paths with in the street. I was headed to the store and on my way there I saw this light skinned girl who was pretty with a big butt walking in my direction. When she passed by, I turned to get another look. She must have been checking me out as well because she turned and caught me staring. We both smiled and she stopped to wait for me to shoot my shot. At that same moment, my pregnant girlfriend was coming around the corner to see my eyes where they had no business being. What was once a bright and beautiful smile, instantly turned into a look of disgust. Something that was intended to be a warm surprise, quickly turned into a cold encounter. Kenniya didn't say anything, she just kept walking and I quickly followed behind her, not caring about the girl I left standing there confused. As soon as I caught up to her, she let me have it. She told me that she was tired of me making her feel second to other women and that I needed to stop risking the family. Again, I tried focusing on my household. I made it my business to bond with my unborn child. By this time I knew that I was having a baby girl. So I would play "Your Beautiful" by Mariah Carey. I talked to and read to her. I already had a name picked out that Kenniya agreed with so I would call her by name. As far as Kenniya, I would give her baths, massage her feet and rub her belly. Since she was eating for two, she wanted food, damn near all the time. I went to the store for snacks as many times as she sent me. Sometimes I would just come in from grocery shopping and she would decide that she would want butter pecan ice cream or crackers and cheese. That means I was right back out the door to fetch all that she requested. Then just like that, we were back to square one. Arguments came all too often and there were a few physical altercations. I tried to be careful not to injure Kenniya, especially since she was pregnant. Every time she was mad, she would attack me and I would do my best to keep things from getting out of hand. She would do something to annoy me and I would give her the "silent treatment". I knew she hated that still, my foolish pride would get in the way. As retaliation she would pack my clothes or she would throw them down the stairs. Kenniya knew how to get under my skin because as soon as I would see my clothes on the floor, I would get up and get in her face and she would swing on me. Sad thing is that I knew all I had to do was just hold her lovingly or tell her something sweet, however I would squeeze her wrists, hoping that she would get the message. During one of our quarrels, I told Kenniya that it seemed as if she liked us to fight. Embarrassment crossed her face, then she said that "it seemed like the only way to get your attention." As soon as the words left her mouth, I instantly felt like shit. I sat down and watched her walk away in silence. The fact that she felt the need to destroy something of mine or hit me, just so I can acknowledge her, said a lot about the relationship and my part in it. The next day I felt even worse because while she was running errands, some high schoolers attacked her. They didn't notice she was pregnant until one of the guys pointed it out. She came home with a gift in her hand and her face distraught, then she proceeded to hand me the gift and said in a low voice *"this is for you"*. I took it and said thank you. I quickly asked with a concerned look on my face "what's wrong?" Kenniya didn't answer, she just broke down and told me the story. Not only did this woman go out and get me something, after I was complete asshole, she caught hell doing it. I felt terrible and helpless. There was nothing I could do. The culprits were long gone by now. I thought to myself, not only do she have to deal with my ass, she had to deal with this. I wanted to find them and chop their hands off, then in the process, find a way to punish myself for ever putting my hands on her. For the rest of that day, I stayed on her hip and tended to her every need. I courted her for about a week, I even tried to seek counseling and asked her to accompany me once or twice. I also found a pastor that we were able to sit down with. We told him about some of our relationship problems. The first thing that came up were the physical altercations. He gave a few suggestions on how to deal with each other during times of stress. I was to walk away but not ignore the problem and she was told not to provoke me. We made it all the way to the birth of our daughter without any other confrontations. The night of Kenniya labor was at the time, satisfying. When she went into labor, no one panicked. We called up one of Kenniya's friend who was close by to give us a ride to the hospital. Though she was having contractions that were close together, she wasn't ready to give birth just yet. Since her cervix wasn't dilated enough, they told her to walk around in the meantime to help with the dilation. Her friend kept an eye on Solace because they didn't allow kids in the emergency room. She stayed with her daughter long enough for Kenniya to get in touch with her mother and ask her to babysit Solace. Mrs. Johnson was to take Solace with her but that changed when she found out I had security stop everyone and allow no one access to Kenniya's room. I knew Kenniya's mother would want to stay and try to be in the room with her however, I wasn't having that. When she arrived, security notified me that someone was in the lobby for us. Since I already knew who it was, I had Solace come with me. The lobby was semi dark though, I still could see Mrs. Washinton's scowl as clear as day. Her gaze pierced my skin and if looks could kill, I would be dead 3x over. I said *"hello"* and then gestured for Solace to go with her. I then proceeded to walk away until I heard her ask, *"why is security stopping me from going in?"* I turned and said *"because I asked them to"*. Her scowl grew harder still, she didn't say anything. I at least wanted her to see Kenniya, so I told her that she could come in, however when it was time for Kenniya to give birth, that I would be the only other person in the room, excluding the staff. I have to admit, I enjoyed seeing her upset. With a blank face, she stared at me for several seconds before walking over to the front desk and complaining to the security guard about not being allowed in the room. She tried to explain how she was the patient's mother and how I wasn't the husband nonetheless, no matter what she said, he still didn't grant her access. When that didn't work, she called Kenniya to ask her how she felt about the situation. Mrs. Johnson isn't getting much out of Kenniya; she was basically undecided. I knew she didn't want to deal with the issue, nor did she want to choose a side. Seemingly frustrated, Mrs. Johnson ended the phone call with *"Ok, call me but I am not taking Solace"*, then she hung up. You might not agree still, I didn't want any negativity in the room while celebrating the birth of my daughter. I felt like even though it was about loved ones coming together for a specific reason, I think the energy would have been off based on reserved feelings. Mrs. Johnson disdain towards me and my animosity towards her would have been in the air. Even though she didn't get to be in the room, I think that she still should have taken Solace. Kenniya had to call the friend back and ask her to watch her daughter. Fortunately for us, she was nice enough to come get Solace. We waited about three hours before Kenniya was ready to give birth. Since the hospital was new, there weren't that many patients there so most of the Doctors and nurses came running into the room. I wanted to protest the amount of people still, I thought it best not to make a scene. I guess there was no time to set Kenniya's leg up on the table because two Doctors just held her legs up. One Doctor holding one leg and the other Doctor holding the other. Kenniya didn't seem uncomfortable with all the people that were there, must have been focused on pushing. I stood on her side and held her hand, while Kenniya huffed and puffed between pushes. Then out she came, a beautiful baby girl. Well, at first, she looked like something out of a horror movie even so, after they wiped her down and her skin settled, she was a sight for sore eyes. I was ecstatic. This was my first time experiencing a birth. I also got to cut the biblical cord which I was certainly nervous about. Maybe the birth of our daughter will bring us closer together and end the madness within our household.

Chapter 11

Be careful what you wish for

A few years before the military, I made my living by cleaning up shelters. I swept, mopped and buffed the floors. It was a good thing I never had to step foot in the bathrooms or rooms because most of NYC shelters are gross. While I was on break, I decided to go outside and walk around. Especially because it was nice out. Amongst all girls that was out, there was one in particular who caught my eye. Shantelle. The future mother of the son that never made it. She was about 5 foot 7, with hair to her shoulders, slim-thick, brown eyes and brown skin. I wasn't really attracted to her nevertheless she had this impressionable look going for her. I knew that she was not yet tainted by men and that I could mold her to my liking. See the problem with females is that after a certain age, they most likely have had several bad experiences with guys. Not to mention one or two heartbreaks. That means it's harder to get in their heads, their hearts and in their beds. Not that I didn't like a challenge, it's just more beneficial for a bachelor to have at least one "good girl" in his corner. Anyway, I found out that she was also a virgin, which was all the better for me. I managed to get her number fairly easy, however talking to her proved to be difficult. I've seen shy before however, Shantelle was a level above that. I had to pull teeth just to get a conversation and if I didn't talk, rest assured she was not talking. It was tough trying to get her to come out her shell but after spending time with her, she started to open up. Shantelle wasn't the only girl that I was dealing with at the time be that as it may I still found the time to go to parties with her, the movies and her house. I never made her my girl; however, I did a lot of boyfriend activities such as exchanging gifts, meeting her family and helping her cut her cake on her birthday. Usually when I date a girl for a little while, she eventually asks me to be her boyfriend or the infamous pre/post sex question "What are we?" Not Shantelle though, she never mentioned anything about it. Even after I took her virginity, she still didn't bring up the topic of us being in a relationship, which was fine by me. Even more, she never once questioned me about other women. Our friendship pretty much stayed like that. Hanging out and having sex. A lot of sex. We started out using protection, until eventually we didn't use anything. That was where I messed up. I got too comfortable to the point that I ejaculated in her. All it took was that one time to change my life forever. Almost two months passed, when I got that dreadful phone call. She told me that she was pregnant. The words didn't phase me though because I had already experienced a few females getting abortions after I had got them pregnant. The sad part is, you would think I would be more careful after it happened the first time but was still being careless and reckless. I calmly explained how we both were young, that she was in school and how I was still getting my life together. I told he she should undergo the procedure, that a baby would slow us down and that it was best for the both of us. Shantelle said that what I was saying made sense however, that she didn't believe in abortions and that she was keeping it. I looked at the phone for a second and then said that in doing so, that she would ruin my plans for the future. She paused for a second and then said that she was sorry that I felt that, regardless of our current situation, that abortion was not an option. It did not matter what I said to Shantelle, her response remained the same. I was frustrated and had enough of trying to convince her so I asked to speak to her mother. When her mother came on, I told her simply that her daughter was pregnant and that she wanted to keep it against my better judgment. Shantelle's mother said that she would take care of it tomorrow. We hung up and I felt like a weight was lifted off of my shoulders. The next day I waited for a phone call of confirmation that never came. I figured since I didn't get a call, she must be too distraught to talk so I decided to call her the next morning. As soon as I woke up, I reached for my phone to check the time and to call her. When she picked up, I said *"Hello...How are you*?" She said that she was fine but I could tell something was off because she sounded nonchalant and her response was extremely dry. I then asked if it was done. She simply replied with "no." I instantly got agitated still, I kept my cool. I asked her why not. The next words out her mouth made my blood boil. She said that she is not getting an abortion, that her mother supported her and that she was going to have it whether I liked it or not. I started to become belligerent, yell obscenities and even threaten her. I told her that I was not going to be around, that she was going to be a single mother and that she was going to regret this for the rest of her life. I even went as far as telling my sister to curse her out for trying to trap me. What surprised me was that Shantelle never raised her voice, used profanity or hung up the phone on me. She kept her cool the whole time, standing her ground. After the call ended, my sister and I never contacted her again. Although I completely distanced myself from her, I still wanted to see the reality of it all, so I stalked her myspace to see what she posted. We weren't friends on myspace so I was only able to see her default picture. I checked her page periodically for about three months before I saw the first picture of her holding her now protruding belly. As the months passed by, so did her default picture of her growing belly. The more I stared at her picture, the more I despised her. No, I would never understand how it feels to have something grow inside of me and yes I was just as responsible for her pregnancy just as much as she was. It was just that I had my life mapped out differently. I was to marry whoever was to bear my child and I wanted to be in love with that woman. I also wanted my child to have certain features that I felt Shantelle did not have. I'm pretty sure I'm not the only person who has had his preferences. Whatever the case, since I didn't love her, that meant there was going to be a second baby but by another woman. So because of ill feelings towards Shantelle, she went her entire pregnancy without hearing so much of a peep from me. I told no one about my situation, not even the girl I was dating at the time. I kept this secret all the way until the birth of my son. Shantelle sent me a picture of a baby, with the words this is your son underneath. My eyes were transfixed on the screen. I didn't move, I just sat there expressionless. A million things went through my head nevertheless, one question kept coming up. What was I to do? I imagined myself acting like it never happened, as if I never received that text of my son's picture, I shook my head at myself for even playing with the idea. How can I in my right mind abandon my responsibilities? How would I be able to live with myself knowing that I have a child that I turned my back on. I decided to forward the message to my friends. Once I sent the last text out, I wanted to tell my mother. I found her sitting in a chair and watching T.V. I stood in front of her and told her that I had something to tell her. She must have sensed my urgency because she had a look of worry on her face. I pulled my phone from my pocket and showed her the picture message. I watched as her eyes scanned the picture, the look of confusion, then the realization that her son had a son. She must have felt dizzy or faint from the news because she fell out of her seat. I ran to her aid and lifted her up off the floor. She didn't say anything, she just kept shaking her head. I started to say something but my phone vibrated in my hand, distracting me. It was my friend asking me what I was going to do. I told him that I didn't know. He didn't text back, instead he called and asked what hospital she was in. When I told him, he told me to get dressed and that he was on his way. Before I knew it he was in front of my house beeping his horn. We got to the hospital about thirty minutes later. It was apparent that the picture she sent was earlier in the day because when we went to the waiting room, Shantelle was still there with her sister. Malik, Shantelle and Shantelle's sister all waved at each other. I on the other hand only said hi to Shantelle's sister. Mostly because she greeted me first, otherwise I would not have said anything at all. I was surprised that she even spoke to me. After all, it has been a little over seven months since I saw or spoke to either of them. I wasn't necessarily expecting the worst however, a dirty look or two would not have been a shock. A few moments later a nurse walked over and said that he can be seen now. When we all stood up, she asked who the father was, I quickly raised my hand. She then said only the mother and father were allowed in the room. I nodded in acknowledgement and waited for her to lead us to the room. Shantelle and I followed her to where he was being held. I walked in to find him in an incubator. Since he was premature he had to spend his time there until he was healthy enough to bring home. I asked a lot of questions concerning his condition and when I was satisfied I started to walk out but before leaving, I put my hand on the machine that he rested in and whispered *"I would never walk out on you again"*. That was the first and last time I saw him. He died a few days later from complications. The things we take for granted.......

Chapter 12

The bed defiled

My newborn Ashley was the most fragile, most crying baby ever. I never knew a baby could cry that much. I've watched people joke about it on T.V. but you don't really know until you experience it on your own. I think it could have been the fact that I made her mother cry a lot while she was pregnant. I read somewhere that babies feel what their mother feels because they are connected through the umbilical cord, so with that said, I felt that I was to blame. I tried to be patient with my bundle of joy, nevertheless the crying would get to me sometimes. Maybe because it was all new to me. Whatever the case, it got to the point where I would ask Kenniya to take her from me to give me a mental break. I would ask while handing her over how come she cries so much. Kenniya would say that it's how babies communicate. Logically it made sense, still her constant cries irritated me. It got to me so much that one day I told Kenniya that our baby girl was annoying. Can somebody slap me please. Out of all the times that I chose to be honest, that was not the moment. There are some things you should never tell a woman, no matter what. For instance, you should never tell your woman that her vagina is not what it used to be. Never tell your woman that she's starting to look old. You definitely should not tell your woman that her sister or friend looks better than her. Most of all you do not tell your woman that her newborn, that she loves dearly is irritating. If she would have punched me, she would not have been wrong. Instead of socking me in my mouth, she yelled at me. She said if that is the case then you reap what you sow. I could not understand why she was so mad, so I told her at least I'm trying to be upfront. Kenniya was so frustrated with me that she ended up calling her mother to tell her what I said. Of course, her mother was just as disgusted as she was by my statement. Kenniya got angrier when she heard her mother say that her stepfather agreed with me. Apparently, he didn't like crying babies either. Kenniya angrily said that she could not stand men and she couldn't stand the sight of me, so she was going to stay at a friend's house for a few days. I didn't care because her absence meant that I could cheat in peace. As soon as I knew that I was in the clear, that was exactly what I did. I invited this sexy Dominican named Genesis over that I knew from New York. I've known her for several years before Kenniya. She knew about Kenniya and our daughter but she still had hope for a future together. It was early in the afternoon when genesis arrived at the station. My neighborhood was predominantly black, that meant she was going to be easily seen. It would not be hard to spot a Latina walking down the block to my house. On top of that Genesis liked to dress sexy whether rain, sleet or shine. I was nervous because I didn't want my neighbors telling Kenniya what I was up to. Genesis called me to tell me that she was close. I stayed on the phone with her while peering out the window. My eyes widened when I saw her, my heart started to race and I felt my blood pressure rise. Genesis was wearing a short black dress. I watched as she looked for the house number I gave her. I watched everybody who was outside stare her down as she passed them. When she was near my porch, I ran downstairs to quickly let her in. As I opened the door I wondered what my neighbors were thinking. Whatever their thoughts were was irrelevant at this point. I shut the door, then hugged her from behind. I wanted her to feel my dick through the sweatpants I wore. She leaned her head back in my chest and said I missed you. I moved her hair to the side so I could kiss her neck then I came from behind her and walked to the living room. Genesis tailed behind me, studying the room as she walked. We sat down on the couch and started talking about the days we were together. We talked for about an hour until my sexual urges got the best of me. I pulled her on top of me and started madly kissing her. She moaned as she returned my kiss with the same intensity. I pulled on Genesis's long black hair, making her head tilt backwards and making her neck more accessible to me. I sucked on her neck like a madman, leaving passion marks when I was done. She was so aroused that she screamed *"I need you inside me now"*. She then hopped off my lap, hiked up her dress and took off her panties. I quickly took off my pants and boxers. She climbed back on top letting me enter the deepest parts of her. We went at it relentlessly, right on the living room floor. I had to lift her up off me several times to keep from losing it. When it came to Genesis, I always had to tell myself "do not nut in her" because every time we had sex she would say while moaning "quiero tener a tu bebe papi." After about three rounds, we were exhausted and ready to lay down. I led her to the bedroom and prepared the bed. Genesis said that she didn't want to get in another woman's bed and that she rather sleep on the floor. I had no choice but to respect her feelings. As I went to grab a comforter and pillow, my conscience started to weigh heavy on me. I felt anger build up inside me. I was angry at myself for bringing her to my home in the first place. I betrayed my relationship, yet again and even worse I betrayed our home. That night, my mind kept me up. I could not sleep at all. I layed there in the dark, just staring at the blackness of the room. I then started to imagine different scenarios. Like what I would do if Kenniya came home. I imagined having to hide her in the closet. I chuckled when the song "Trapped in the closet" played in my head. I didn't really know what would happen if Kenniya caught her in here nonetheless, I did know I did not want to find out. As soon as the sun came up, I tapped Genesis on the shoulder and when she awoke, I told her that she had to go. She quickly got herself together and left. Once she had gone, I cleaned the house, washed the dishes and texted Kenniya to see how she was doing. She texted back saying that she was ok and that she was coming home later. I played my game until Kenniya and the girls arrived. When they walked in, for some reason I never moved from where I was. I just turned off the game and turned my body towards the door. Solace ran in and gave me a hug. As I held her, I realized why I didn't get up. I was feeling shameful and the more I looked at the girls, the more I felt like crap. I wasn't just betraying Kenniya or our home for that matter, I was also betraying the two little girls who I called "daughters". When I finally got up, I walked over to Kenniya and gestured for the baby. She put Ashley in my arms then walked upstairs. I rocked her and kissed her face while Solace talked to me about her visit. Then suddenly sorrow washed over me and my eyes watered up. That was when I vowed that Genesis would be the last woman that I would have over. Unfortunately, she was not.

Chapter 13

Impudence

They say home is where the heart is and that your home should be a sanctuary. They also say "don't shit where you eat". So that means one should respect their place of residence as well as someone else's. That all sounds good still, what does that mean to someone who values and morals are as short as their temper. At a young age I dealt with a handful of females who had their own place. A couple of them I actually lived with for a short period of time. The very first woman I started staying with was the first woman that I violated. She was this pretty brown skinned Jamaican named Yolanda. She was a freshman in college and when Yolanda would go to school, I would desecrate her home. I had a total of four girls come to her house and I was working on a fifth. All of which I had sex with in her bed. The disrespect didn't stop there. I would even go as far as asking them to try on her dresses, saying that the dresses were my sister's and I just wanted to see how they fit. It was just a ploy to make the goodies easily accessible. The second girl I did it to stayed with her parents. Both parents worked morning schedules. While they were at work, she was in class. One day, she gave me her keys and told me to wait at her house until she got out of school. I misused her act of trust by bringing a girl to her house. Which was the same girl I tried to bring to Yolanda house. This time I got caught before I did anything. Brittany's grandparents walked in the house before I got to make my move. Apparently, they had keys too and were picking something up. As soon as they walked in, they gave me and the girl sitting next to me a suspicious look. Talk about awkward. I waved with a stupid grin on my face, grabbed the girl and just left. I knew I was getting sloppy when my cover was blown three more times. Remember Genesis? The same Dominican that came to see me in Jersey. Well, she had an apartment in Brownsville projects. She worked in a supermarket nearby, so I don't know why I took the risk of bringing someone to her house in the first place. It was a Sunday morning when she got the phone call to come to work. I remember it being that specific day because the girl I got busted with came to see me after church. I was just finishing up having sex when I heard a knock at the door. My eyes widened and my heart sank. Jennifer looked at me confusingly, waiting for answers that I didn't have. I just froze, hoping that it wasn't Genesis. I gestured for Jennifer to be quiet while peering out the window. A few seconds later I saw Genesis walking out the building. I didn't move until I saw her turn the corner. When I thought the coast was clear, I had my still naked companion get dressed as fast as humanly possible. I let her out soon after, only to find a Hispanic boy sitting adjacent to the apartment. I stuck my head back in and locked the door. I shook my head because I knew Genesis purposely placed him there. All I could think was "damn that was smart". Moments later Genesis was at the door. I took a deep breath before opening it. Her only words were *"get your stuff and leave"*. I tried to do damage control by feeding her bull shit apologies and empty promises. When it didn't seem like it was working, I threatened to beat up whoever that boy was. She said *"my cousin is long gone"*. I felt myself getting angry to the point that if I found him, I would have done some real damage. Thank GOD I caught myself before I did something stupid. I wondered why in the world I was even mad. The fact that I even had the audacity to be upset, puzzled me. The last two times I was discovered were not as dramatic. One of the two was the same girl I brought over to Genesis house. No one had a pass. Not even the one I cared for the most. The most despicable out of the two was with the first girl I snuck over before Genesis. Renee was her name. I met her while I was visiting my mother in queens. She was smaller than I usually go for but she had a tight body. In just a few days of getting to know each other, I was already trying to infiltrate her home.

However, after finding out that she didn't live by herself and rarely had any privacy, I was left with only two choices. Either invite her over the place I shared with Kenniya or take her to a hotel. I made the decision to bring her over to the house because Kenniya was out with her friend for the day. When Renee came over I already knew that she was going to give me "some" so I did not mention sex or come on to her. Instead, I suggested for us to play strip poker. I knew that if she was game, no matter who loss, the outcome would be the same. Renee agreed as planned and to my surprise she had beginners luck. I was in my boxers within five minutes. All she lost was her top which exposed her red lace bra. Still, it was more than enough to make a move. I took her hand and led her upstairs to my bedroom. I removed her pants to reveal matching panties. I smiled inwardly, thinking that she was prepared for this. I backed up for a better view of her body. Renee looked like a "fun size" chocolate treat. I wanted to gobble her up and that I did. After we were done, we just layed there in silence, still high off of sex. I then got up to use the bathroom but made sure that I took my phone so I could check in on Kenniya. We spoke briefly on how we were doing however, her next few words bought me down from my high and was replaced by fear. Kenniya said that she was on her way. My adrenaline started pumping and my brain started to come up with different scenarios on what would happen if we got caught. I could not let that happen. Renee had to go. I had about 15mins tops I thought. I must of looked spooked when I came out the bathroom because a look of worry crossed her face. She asked what was wrong and I nervously said that my brother was shot. I said it again but in a more frantic tone, to add to the effect. I never was the type to kick a girl out or leave after sex. I believed in seconds however, this was an emergency. got dressed in record time and hysterically asked her to get dressed too. I ran downstairs to put on my sneakers as well as gather up all her belongings. When she came downstairs, I ran upstairs to make sure there was not anything left to raise suspension. I quickly scanned the room for underwear and strands of hair. After I felt satisfied that I removed all evidence, I quickly grabbed Renee and left the house. My nerves started to get to me and I started to go into panic mode. As we were walking, my eyes were all over the place as if I had people after me. I just kept thinking "I can not be seen with this girl". The train was a ten minute walk and I needed every last one of them to scan over the house again. I started to slow down after the second block. Thoughts started to crowd my mind like "what would be my excuse for being out of the house at this time of night?" When I came up with no logical answer, I slowed down even more. I didn't even care if she noticed even so, she just kept walking if she did. Before we crossed the street to the third block, I yelled out *damn I forgot my gun, keep walking, I'll catch up to you*". I ran like a track star back to the house. I busted in like somebody was chasing me, put back on my night clothes and silenced my phone. Kenniya came in about four minutes after me. While I helped Kenniya and the kids settle in, I prayed that Renee was not curious or concerned enough to come back and see what was taking me so long. Not long after, Renee texted me and asked if I was coming. I told her that I was and that it took me a while to find the weapon. After about a minute, she texted again saying that she was getting on the train without me. I sighed with relief. I texted back "ok" then turned off my phone. Good thing Kenniya was too tired to pay attention to my subtleties. I got in the bed with her, frowning at my reckless behavior. Though I was sure Renee left, I stayed awake for about an half hour just to be certain. I finally fell asleep, telling myself that I needed to stop getting into these types of situations. Hopefully, I'll listen to me.

Chapter 14

Calamity

John Legend said "Everybody knows but nobody really knows how to make it work". I felt that in my toes. A lot of people will tell you key things for making a relationship work and everybody seemingly is an expert. Family, friends and coworkers pretend to have all the answers but when it comes to their own life, they're clueless. Truth is, we are all trying to figure it out as we go. It's just that some of us are better at figuring it out than others. I was getting tips and tools about relationships from people who contradicted what they were telling me. I decided to seek spiritual advice. This is when that pastor from chapter 10 comes in. I didn't necessarily grow up in a church however, I definitely went to church throughout my years. I took to the teachings and the gospel. So naturally when I find myself without answers, I go to what I know. For me, the preacher and the choir have to be good. If the pastor preached well but the choir is dull, most likely I'm not coming back. In this particular church, I liked the pastor, still I was not fond of the choir. Let's just say the choir members and the music was vintage. The only reason why I kept going back was to speak to the pastor. I don't know what was to come of the talk, I just knew I needed to hear him and try before I lost what was dear to me. I don't care what anybody says, we all know when our relationships are on their last legs. We either make the decision to change the course of the direction of our relationship or watch it burn to the ground. Relationships are like owning a home. If you don't make payments on it, you go into default. You still have sufficient time to rectify your situation but then there is foreclosure and the chances of getting your house back after that is slim to none. That is when your house can be bought by somebody else. That means, no matter how much money, time and effort that you have put into it, your house can belong to somebody else. We have to understand that there will be bumps along the way however, we also have to make sure that we make conscious decisions to lessen them. In my case I needed patience and a lot of understanding because Kenniya and I were holding on by a thread. She told me that I would have to carry her for a while. That meant she was not going to spend as much time and energy trying to fix it as before. She said that she was no longer going to fight, beg or put any real effort in trying to make it work anymore. One of the worst things you can experience in a relationship after heartbreak, is having to be the one to do all the work. I was now the one "pulling teeth" running behind her. I was pretty much the only one who was trying to put the pieces of our relationship back together again. I have to admit that I do not know how women do some of the things they do. Like putting up with us men. I was ready to quit every week. I kept asking Kenniya to meet me halfway but she was not budging. I kept coming up with different solutions for us, still they all failed miserably. I knew where Kenniya stood as far as her feelings for me because her toleration for anything was basically gone. We all have different sides to us. This was the first time that I saw a different side of Kenniya. The ugly side. There was this one night where Kenniya and I were beefing and we really weren't talking to each other. I was in NY shopping and trying to get a grip on things. I figured the time away would help. I headed back to NJ about 8pm and made it to the house about 10:30pm. Before I even walked in the door, I noticed a lit black & mild on the window seal. I never liked the smell of them so I quickly threw it out but not before mentally preparing myself for what was next. I walked in the house to find Kenniya and her known "friend" sitting in the living room. Kenniya was sitting on the loveseat holding our baby girl and he was on the sofa playing with our dog. I was hot all over, still somehow I managed to keep my composure. It's not like I haven't met him before, it was the fact that he was there at that hour. The first thing I did was turn off the T.V and in a stern voice, I told her friend Tre that he had to go. He promptly got up, said his farewells to Kenniya and headed for the door. As soon as he made his exit, I asked Kenniya why he was here at this time of night. She said that she needed pampers, that she didn't want to bother me so she figured she would ask for help. She then added that she felt embarrassed because here I am walking in with shopping bags but no pampers. While we were busy arguing, Tre called her phone. I gave Kenniya a look that told her not to move. At this point I was not as calm as before. I took her phone and answered it, Tre paused for a moment when he realized it was me. He then asked me what happened to his black & mild. In an irritated voice, I told him I had thrown it out. I had to give this man points for bravery because he actually had the balls to tell me that I needed to replace it. I sarcastically told him to wait on it. Then in a low menacing tone, I said *"don't let me catch you in here again"* and hung up angrier than before. I knew if I saw him again, I was going to hurt that man. I looked up at Kenniya who was now standing up holding our daughter. In a fit of rage I kicked the garbage and punched two holes in our living room wall. Kenniya watched me cautiously while I threw a temper tantrum. I asked her *"how messed up is our relationship that you could not call me to tell me that our daughter needed pampers?"* Her only rebuttal was that she didn't think that I would answer. I then asked "you didn't think a text would suffice?" She said that she wasn't thinking and that the only thing on her mind was that Ashley needed pampers. In the back of my mind, I knew she did that on purpose. Women can be vindictive. I decided to take on the chin because I felt that the rift in our relationship was my fault. Besides, our daughter did need pampers and I should have known that our daughter was without. Still, my anger would not subside. I just kept thinking about this man inside my home and possibly my woman. I called one of my female friends to be petty and vent. I started telling her in detail, all that had happened. Kenniya was furious. I know I had to be careful though because when

Kenniya was mad, she was dangerous. As I talked, I kept my eyes trained on her. She calmly walked downstairs for what seemed like ten minutes. When she finally reappeared, she had apparently left our daughter in her spare crib. Not only that, she had a glass bottle in one hand and bleach in her other hand. I wanted to go downstairs but I dared not to move from my position. My opportunity came when she suddenly turned on her heels and went back downstairs. I quickly crept to the doorway to make sure she had gone, then I looked over the banister and saw that my clothes were piled up on the floor. That was when it dawned on me, that the bleach was for my clothes. I dared not leave from upstairs though, instead I just told my friend what I discovered. I heard Kenniya coming and immediately ran for cover. When she came back into the room, I said out loud that "my ex was acting crazy", knowing that it would piss Kenniya off. She showed me how much she did not appreciate my comment by punching me square in the nose. I'm not going to lie, she made my eyes water. I got off the phone and quickly grabbed Kenniya's hand before she could strike again. We had a brief stare down before I let her go. She momentarily exited the room yet came back with the same glass bottle that she had earlier. With a crazed look in her eyes, Kenniya suddenly broke the glass bottle on the dresser then lunged at me. I jumped back and grabbed both her wrists and started trying to shake the broken glass bottle out of her hands. Our scuffle stopped when I noticed blood dripping down her chest. Apparently, she accidently cut herself during the altercation. I bolted to the bathroom to get peroxide, a paper towel and some band aids. Since I could not find the peroxide in the bathroom upstairs, I turned and darted downstairs. On the way to the bathroom, I noticed two pots of boiling water in the kitchen and a bunch of China plates on the living room couch. I shook my head at the scene and continued looking for the peroxide and made haste back upstairs. Kenniya was just sitting on the bed with her head down. I kneeled in front of her, lifted her chin and started tending to her wound. Thank goodness it was not bad enough for her to need stitches. Once I was done, I sat next to her and could not stop shaking my head at the whole situation. I finally broke the silence by asking her what the pots of boiling water and China dishes were for. Kenniya just looked at me with crazed eyes, letting me know that she had diabolical plans for me. I didn't speak to her for the rest of the night. I didn't even want to be next to her so I slept on the couch. I knew that she didn't like for me to sleep apart from her, however, at the moment I didn't care. That was my usual way of handling our disputes. Separating myself from her and shutting down. I tried to sleep, yet my brain was on over time. Was she really going to burn me with hot water like we were in a Medea movie? What would have happened if she didn't cut herself? Would she be satisfied if I had been cut instead? What was she going to Frisbee the China dishes for me? Then I started plotting my evening with my friends and how I was going to get this girl named Lucinda to bed. The altercation between Kenniya and I, fueled the lust that was already in me. That same night Kenniya came downstairs to "kiss and make up" with me nonetheless, despite her best efforts, I still would not give in. Pride, stubbornness and lechery just would not let me budge. Even as she literally pleaded from her knees, I continued to lay on my side with my back towards her. Still, she repeatedly asked for my forgiveness. When Kenniya finally had enough of my "cold shoulder" she defeatedly got up and cried all the way to the bedroom. I forced myself to sleep, hating the fact that I really wanted to just tell her that I was sorry. Now I know the saying is true. "You should never go to bed angry".

Chapter 15

Forbidden Fruit

Lucinda was a childhood crush. She was several years older than me so in my mind she was out of my league. I still played with the idea that her and I would eventually hit it off. Lucinda was this sassy, sexy and sultry Puerto Rican. Standing at 5'7 with jet black hair and bright hazel eyes. She was slim but her curves were hazardous. She had light skin and sex appeal that had its own gravitational pull. Even though I admired Lucinda, I did so from a distance. She was off limits. She was the sister of one of the older guys who used to hustle for my cousin in those days. He was one of the many guys around the way that looked after my friends and I while we terrorized the streets. Ronaldo was crazy even so, he also was fun. He would let us come over to his family house to play video games with him. It was a two family house. His mother and father stayed downstairs, while Ronaldo and his sister lived upstairs. Every now and again we would see Lucinda come in and out of the house. As she passed we would watch in awe at all her beauty. Every last one of us wished that we had a chance with her. We even playfully fought one another about who girlfriend she would become. Lucinda on the other hand, paid us no mind since we were little boys to her. She would wear house clothes that would show off her body. Like shirts with no bras or little pajama shorts accentuating her perky breasts and ample bottom. That was her normal attire if she was just chilling at home. Sometimes she would leave her room door open while she was doing her makeup or just laying on the bed. There were about seven of us; however, only four could play at a time. Whenever I wasn't playing, I would go to the bathroom or raid the refrigerator, just to see her. At first Lucinda didn't give any of us a second look, nevertheless the older we got the more she paid attention. Now instead of us finding reasons to be around her, it seemed she would find reasons to be around us. Whether it was asking if we were hungry or asking what game we were playing, Lucinda was bound to pop up. Whenever Ronaldo wasn't around, we would make passes at her. I think he knew she was into us because he would make sure that we were never alone with her for too long. Still, he could not stop the inevitable. Some years later, my friend Roman started dating her. Then they went on and had two kids together. By this time, we all had lives of our own so we didn't see each other as often. We mostly would meet up for birthdays and certain events. Several years had passed since we saw Roman. Mainly because he moved away with his family. We still kept in touch on Facebook though and would see him post pictures of his training. He invited us to his fight via Facebook so of course we all went to support. Even after not seeing us for some time, it felt like yesterday. We didn't miss a beat. Greeting each other enthusiastically. Then someone caught my eye. It was Lucinda coming up from behind, looking no older than she did when we saw her last. She gave us all hugs and asked us how we were doing. Although I was still attracted to Lucinda, I respected her relationship. I kept it strictly platonic. Lucinda on the other hand was very flirtatious. I'm not sure if she knew what she was doing or maybe she did nevertheless it made me wonder if things were ok at home. I knew she thought that I was attractive because she would state it. There was this one time Roman posted a picture of all of us and she commented underneath the picture saying "handsome guys". Also she would purposely find excuses to touch me. She would playfully elbow me or would make sure that I hugged her when we all got together. The more I saw her the closer her and I got. We eventually exchanged numbers and started calling each other. She would tell me about things that I had no business knowing unless Roman had told me. It didn't take long for Roman to get wind of our new "friendship". Lucinda would tell me that Roman felt some type of way and that she was stealing "his" friend away. I would start to feel bad but then she would always say "if Roman is your friend, how come he doesn't call you?" She would then add the fact that he hardly even asked about me. I thought that eventually Roman would approach me about the friendship that was developing between Lucinda and I yet, he never did. It made what I was about to do next easier. I decided to find out if her flirting was harmless or if she was sending me signals this whole time. Since I didn't want to look stupid by asking straight up, I had to find a way to get my message across while still leaving me cushion room just in case I read her wrong. I decided to send her an "accidental dick pic." Bracing myself for her reaction, I laughed at myself and thought of all the possible outcomes. Lucinda replied via text message asking if the picture was for her. I told her no and that I apologized for my error. She then asked for the name of the person that it was for. Thinking on my feet, I thought of an old girlfriend's name and said "Lacey". Her only response was "OMG OMG OMG...LOL". I didn't want to press the conversation so I left it there. I figured I would wait until the next day to text her again. The following evening I asked Lucinda how she was doing. She said that she was fine however, aside from that, that she could not get that image off of her mind. I now knew that I had a chance to "hook up" with Lucinda if there was ever an opportunity. It just so happened that the opportunity was coming sooner than later. I was having a birthday party at a club and I invited all my boys, some girls and Lucinda. The day of my party, my boys and I rode together to where the event was being held and we were the first ones to arrive. It didn't take long for everybody else to show up. I didn't think I would be as excited as I was, however, when Lucinda finally came through the door, I was ecstatic. I played it cool though because I did not want to seem anxious, especially because Roman was there. I mingled with everybody, accepting the drinks that they offered me along the way. Lucinda was watching me from afar and when I made my way closer to where she sat, she ordered us a drink. She seemed determined to get me drunk because she started mixing our liquor. After a few rounds I started feeling inebriated so I went to get some air. As time went on, my guests gradually started leaving wishing me a happy birthday on their way out including Roman and his brother. That left just Lucinda and me. It didn't take long for her to take full advantage of the situation. She led me to the dance floor and started dancing the moment we found a spot. She was swaying, rotating and moving in a very seductive way. I danced with her, letting our bodies harmonize on the floor. My hands traveled along the surface of her curves, making her gyrate on me even harder. Our rhythm and sensuality must have been alluring because three other women joined us. I was now surrounded by four gorgeous women who were taking turns grinding on me. While I danced with one woman, the others would dance with each other. It went on like that for half of a song. Then the women left but not before giving Lucinda their number. She smiled at them, then walked up to me, looked me square in the eyes and kissed my neck. I understood that to be universal for "she's ready for action". We left the dance floor and headed for the door. Lucinda requested that I drive her car because she was too intoxicated to drive herself. What she failed to realize was that I was just as drunk as her. Thinking that I could manage, I got behind the wheel and attempted to drive to the nearest hotel. I drove until I could not drive anymore. My vision was blurred so I pulled over to avoid getting into a car accident or worse. When I turned to tell Lucinda that we were going to have to stay where we were at, she was already climbing to the backseat. I turned off the car, pulled the front seats up, then quickly joined her. As soon as I got comfortable, Lucinda started to close the distance between us. At first we kissed, slow and steady then after a few seconds, we were making out like horny teenagers. I started to lift her dress up, revealing that she didn't have any underwear on. In one quick motion, I picked up and had her straddle my legs. We began kissing with the same energy as before. She reached down to unzip my pants and grabbed my fully erect penis. I lifted her up a little so I could pull my pants and boxers down to my ankles. Then she guided herself on my shaft, letting me feel how wet she was. I cupped her soft buttocks while she rode me. We went at it like a scene from a movie, fogging up the windows. Although there was not a lot of room, I was still able to maneuver around like I was a pro at "car sex". Once Lucinda leaned back and screamed *"I'm cumming papi"* I lost it. I pulled her hair as she convulsed and trembled while releasing thirteen years worth of fantasy inside of her. How small of me to think that I actually accomplished something. There are no awards for sleeping with your boy's baby mother. Shortly after, we both fell asleep in the back seat of her car. The rising of the sun ended our slumber. She told me to take her to her brother's house. Lucinda and I rode back in silence, mutually not wanting to talk about what had happened between us. When we arrived at the house, she told me that we needed to talk later. I nodded in agreement and then headed for home. She called me that afternoon, telling me that she did not want anyone to know what went down in the backseat of her car. We vowed not to tell a soul and to end things before it got out of hand. That was the last day we spoke face to face. She would tell me that she could not trust herself around me and that talking to me made her want seconds and thirds. Since we knew that our affair was inevitable, it was easier to stop talking all together. It was an unspoken agreement. We just suddenly stopped calling each other. It was for the best. Imagine if I had got her pregnant, that would have been ugly. Talking to the opposite sex when you and your mate are going through it, is dangerous, especially when you're attracted to them.....I don't care what nobody says.

Chapter 16

Damaged Goods

A broken man and a damaged woman should not be together. It is a recipe for disaster. Unless healing takes place, it will never work. I had pint up anger which was often misdirected. I was the type of person that when I'm angered, I distance myself. I was never one to argue, I rather just leave. Kenniya on the other hand had to, needed to talk it out. She would follow me wherever I tried to escape. She would yell, scream and shout until I caved. Then when that didn't work, she would go ballistic or just cry. Most times I would not budge and the more I resisted the more she would purposely irritate me. I would try to not allow her to get to me. I would try to show restraint still, there were a few times where I didn't. One of those times was the worst it had ever been. Kenniya and I weren't seeing eye the eye yet again, so I simply just wanted to remove myself from the situation. I wanted to seclude myself. I went into the basement to get away from the static and to calm my nerves. While I was collecting my thoughts, I heard Kenniya walk towards the basement door and instantly was perturbed. It surprised me when I noticed that she wasn't coming down. She just touched the knob and walked away. Kenniya was very spiteful, so something wasn't feeling right. After about two minutes, it dawned on me that she must have locked the door. I took a deep breath to calm my nerves before heading to the door. I fiddled with the knob, confirming the obvious. Then I knocked on the door, calling her name repeatedly. I started to get mad all over again. The more I knocked and called her name, the angrier I became. I was enraged and my whole body was hot. I ended up kicking down the door looking like a madman. Kenniya looked at me with wide eyes, obviously startled by my antics. I didn't want to hurt her; I just wanted her to see my frustrations. I stepped over the broken pieces of wood, trying to hold back the anger that was rising inside of me. For a moment I just stared at her menacingly while she just stood there stuck in her tracks. Without warning, I charged at her, blindly pushing her back. She lost her balance and fell into the living room wall. After her collision, she fell to the floor and started coughing. I couldn't immediately see even so, I knew I shoved her way too hard. Truthfully, I should not have shoved her at all. Remorse filled the spaces that anger was holding and I was genuinely concerned. With worry on my face, I went to aid, praying that she was o.k. I wasn't exactly sure what part of her body initially hit the wall, so I looked her over, making sure that she didn't have any bumps or bruises. Once I was done examining her, I retrieved a rag and a pillow. I wiped her mouth, then I gently rested her head on the pillow. As I tended to her, my eyes started to water. I asked, *"are you ok?"* In a low voice, she said *"yes"*, relieving me a little. Just to be sure, I asked again and again, yet she still gave me the same answer each time. I carefully lifted her up, walked over to the couch and gently laid her down. Overwhelmed by guilt, I kneeled beside her and silently cried. As the tears rolled down my face, I thought of this movie called "He got game". There was this scene where a father and son were squabbling with each other. The mother intervenes by trying to get in between them. The father, in the heat of the moment, blindly shoves the mother off him and she falls back, hitting her head on the kitchen counter. She dies instantly. The father had to endure the death of his wife by his own hands and the disdain from his son. Having to live with something like that would be extremely excruciating. I can't imagine accidently killing Kenniya and then explaining to my child what I did to her mother. The next day, I asked Kenniya to make an appointment for a general checkup. I had to be certain that she was in good health. I thought that some positive results would give me some peace of mind, though even when she told me that she was all good, my spirit was still troubled. I was plagued with a question that kept playing in my head. "What if?" What if it had gone further? What if I had to spend most of my life behind bars? What if the last words that I heard from my daughter's mouth were "I hate you?" It constantly crossed my mind. I thought about it at work, at the dinner table, in the shower etc... Time had passed and even though Kenniya and I were doing better, I just could not escape those thoughts. It got to the point that it started to affect my work. Around this time, I was No longer Active duty, I was now Army National Guard and was working for a fish distribution company. My job was to deliver fish and fill out some paperwork. As easy as that was, I still found a way to mess that up. Time after time I would make some errors on the paperwork. I just could not focus on anything except that frightful night. Eventually, I lost my job and since I was the only one working, I was stressed out even more. We didn't have enough savings to sustain us, so I had to find a job soon. I was able to land a job after going to several interviews, however it wasn't soon enough. Unfortunately, we lost the house as a result. That was one of the toughest things that I ever had to experience in my life. It wasn't just because we lost the house. It was because we were splitting up and it was all my fault. We had to pack up all of our belongings, which was done in silence. There wasn't much to talk about. We had already discussed that she was going back to her mother's house and that I was going to have to live with my sister. Also, I had promised Kenniya that I was going to fix our current predicament. So, nothing was said the entire time we packed. Kenniya called one of her friends to help us load her stuff in a U-Haul truck. Once we had finished, the plan was for her friend to take the U-Haul to the drop off location and Kenniya was to follow behind her. For the most part we kept our emotions contained but once we finally looked at each other, it all came out. Kenniya started to sob while tears flowed down my eyes. I held her in my arms and we both just cried. I then kissed both of her eyes and told her that it was only temporary. I let her go, then opened her door for her to get in. As I watched the three of them drive off, I told myself that it was going to work out in the end. I wondered if I even believed myself.

Chapter 17

Typhoon

New York City. The home of the bold and the brave. My home.
Still, I felt out of place. For starters, I was now living in a house
with three of my sisters, three of their kids and my mother. I
slept on the couch in the living room. 3 bedrooms and 2
bathrooms was not enough space to accommodate everyone.
The only upside to my situation was that I was around family.
Being there was somewhat of a distraction from reality but
when the night came, I greatly missed the family that I created.
Speaking to Kenniya and the kids everyday didn't help. In fact,
it made it worse. The holidays were approaching fast and
Kenniya wanted me to have things situated before Christmas.
On top of that my stepdaughter already had a Christmas list.
She told me that the only two things that she wanted was a
teddy bear and for us to be a family again. Her requests
instantly made my eyes water. It never occurred to me that my
step-daughter was also affected by the separation. She started to
tell me how much she missed me and wished that we all could
be together. Even at five years old this little girl was able to
articulate her feelings. I promised her that I would do my best
to get her all that she wanted. Honestly, I really wasn't even
sure if I could keep that promise, let alone by Christmas. A few
days later one of the worst hurricanes hit NYC. A Category 3
named Sandy. Sandy killed over 280 people, causing nearly 70
billion in damages. There were many homes destroyed and so
many people in need of aid that the National Guard, FEMA and
other emergency responders were called in. We all were staged
at Floyd Bennett Field in Brooklyn. I can't say for sure what
everyone was assigned to do, however as for my unit, we were
to deliver supplies to various places. We transported water,
blankets, food etc... Everybody worked around the clock,

sleeping only a few hours at a time. There were times that a mission would come down in the wee hours of the morning, so we had to be ready at a moment's notice. There were tents though, some of us would sleep in tactical vehicles. I played my part without any hiccups but about a month in I started to find myself in trouble. Mainly because I was extremely stressed. I was missing my family and my family was missing me. Not to mention, Christmas was approaching fast and I wasn't any closer to finding us a house. In addition, Kenniya was having recurring nightmares about me. I wanted her to dream about me but never in this way. She told me that in her dream, she seen all the men that raped and molested her. She explained that they slowly surrounded her while she called for me but when I finally appeared it was to only tell her that I could not save her. I'll tell you something that really messed with me mentally. The fact that I knew every detail of her past made me feel disgusted with myself. I didn't rape her or sexually assault her nevertheless, I was supposed to be the difference. In a world full of disappointment, mistreatment and heartbreak, Kenniya expected that I would show her something new. She trusted me, loved me and let her guard completely down, to the point that she dreamed about it in the most horrifying way. I was angry, angry at myself and it started to show. I started to act out by disrespecting my leadership. I got into two separate altercations. One of them led to me losing rank. My first incident was with a safety officer. I was driving a Humvee while talking on the phone. Not only that, I also did not have a seatbelt on, I was not wearing a helmet, I was speeding and didn't even have my headlights on. I was an Article 15 waiting to happen. It didn't take long for someone to spot me. I was seen by an NCO on patrol. He was driving past me in a Humvee and as soon as he saw me, he quickly made a "U" turn. He then flashed his head lights, signaling for me to stop. I pulled over to the side, trying to brace myself for what was to come. I told Kenniya that I had to call her back, then I anxiously waited for the safety officer to get out of his vehicle and approach mine. When he came over, he ordered me to get out. I complied and since he was an NCO, I stood in front of him at "parade rest". He chewed me out, pointing out everything that I did wrong. All I could say was "Roger". After he was done, he ordered me to take the Humvee back where I got it from. I snapped to "attention" and proceeded to do as I was told. He then yelled with the ugliest of attitudes for me to leave Humvee and come back with a helmet. It was very cold out and I still was about a little more than a half mile away from the tent, so I had to be sure of what he was telling me. I asked, *"so you want me to walk all the way back to my tent in this weather?"* With a nastier attitude he replied *"exactly"*. My restraint was crumbling fast still, I was holding on to the ounce I had left. I said in a low stern voice *"you're starting to piss me off"*. He responded by saying *"your feelings were never a factor in this equation"*. That was it for me. I walked up to him, inches from his face and said to him *"now you can kick rocks pussy"*. He just smiled and told me that he liked getting soldiers in trouble. I wanted him to push me or say something disrespectful so I could have an excuse to whip his ass but he never did. I turned, got in the Humvee and drove away in frustration. As I calmed down, I shook my head at myself, knowing that it was just a matter of time before that run in with the Patrol officer would come back to bite me on the ass. The next day my supposition came true. I was approached by my team leader and platoon Sergeant, asking about what occurred last night between me and a safety officer. I told them everything, detail for detail. I also added that I was extremely stressed because of my personal life, however I did not get into why. I just wanted them to know that I was not myself. As a result, my platoon Sergeant ordered me to stay on my team leader's hip. That meant I had to go wherever he went and worst of all, I had to sleep next to him. I felt like I was on suicide watch. I could not stand it. Several of my comrades were asking me why they put me on a leash, which only made me more upset. I had to speak to someone quick before I exploded. I decided it was best that I speak to a Chaplain. I told him all that was going on with me. I talked about Kenniya, her dreams, my unit and what was happening. He basically told me that I was on a road to self-destruction. I did not understand what he really meant by that until I got myself into another altercation.

Chapter 18

The storm within

Floyd Bennet's field had a lot of moving parts. Military vehicles coming in and out, FEMA trucks loading supplies and emergency vehicles making their rounds. Everybody was in motion except me. On the outside, I seemed alright. I went out with the fellas after our missions, I laughed, joked and was seemingly merry. However, on the inside I was in turmoil. Kenniya was still having that same nightmare. My only solution was for her to call me when it happened, no matter the time of night. I also would try to stay on the phone with her until she fell asleep. Most times I answered when she called though, there were a few that I missed. The nights that I would drink with the guys were the nights that I slept the hardest. I would wake up to a bunch of missed calls, a handful of texts and a few voicemails. I always was nervous before reading and listening to her messages because I knew it would make me feel worse than I already was feeling. Most of the messages were her texting "please wake up", asking me if I was sleeping or asking about my whereabouts. The voice mails were more intense. They consisted of Kenniya crying and reminding me of my promise to pick up no matter what. Once I read and listened to all her messages, I would call soon after with an explanation, a few sorry's and I love you's. It killed me to not be able to be with her, to hold and console her. I wanted to be able to kiss her forehead and tell her that "it would be O.K". Since I couldn't physically be there for her, I walked around feeling heavy because of the chip on my shoulder. Truthfully, I was a pipe, ready to burst, it was just a matter of time. Sure enough, that time came around. One of my comrades got into a heated argument with an NCO named Sergeant Rodriguez. Before it got out of hand another NCO decided to intervene. His attempt was a total failure because instead of properly defusing the situation, he was mocking them. Sergeant Rodriguez was making me angry by the way he was handling the dispute as NCO. Once I was fed up with him instigating, I stepped in to defuse the situation myself. I told Sergeant Rodriguez to back off and then told my battle buddy to calm down. As I'm helping my buddy reel it back in, I overhear Sergeant Rodriguez mocking me too. Since I didn't like him anyway, that was all I needed to send me over the edge. I quickly turned towards his direction and gave him a look that could kill. I picked up my helmet, insisting that he do it again. I waited in anticipation for him to mock me, mimic me or anything really so I could hit him with the helmet that I held. To my disappointment, he never said a word. Instead, he watched me for several seconds, then left me standing there, looking stupid. A few hours later I was still fuming. I had to take a walk, or I was going to end up taking my frustrations out on an undeserving soul. I made sure that I wasn't on rotation for any missions before I went anywhere. I took a cab to the liquor store to find a bottle to drown my sorrows in. I went back to the tent and waited for the traffic to slow down. I then found a secluded space and started drinking. Around 1:00am, my phone rang but I did not look at it, nor did I answer because I already knew who it was. I was not in a place to deal with Kenniya at that moment. There was no way that I could even hold a conversation after drinking half of the 750ml Jack Daniels (Whiskey) I had. In addition, I knew that I was not in the mental space to handle her emotions. Thank goodness Kenniya only called once that night so I was not pressured to answer the phone. I drank some more then tossed the rest in the woods. I then walked back to my tent trying my best to walk in a straight line. I made it back without being discovered and fell asleep on my cot. The next day, I woke up with the worst hangover I have ever had. I went to breakfast with my head down and my eyes barely open. I sat alone, eating slowly, hoping that I would not throw it back up. I forgot all about the altercation between Sergeant Rodriguez and

I. In fact, I thought that was the end of it, however that wasn't the case at all. Sergeant Rodriguez went to our platoon Sergeant and told him what occurred between him and I. They decided to give me an Article 15 for disrespecting an NCO. As soon as I left the chow hall, a private was waiting to escort me to our headquarters. I marched behind my escort in silence while my head seemed like it was going to explode. Sergeant Rodriguez and my platoon Sergeant were already waiting for me with documents in their hands. My head hung low, not from embarrassment or shame but because I was trying to hide my hangover. My platoon Sergeant read the article that was to remove my rank. He then asked for the patch that rested in the middle of my chest. He replaced it with a lower rank and handed me those same papers to sign. I left thinking that I could no longer allow someone to control my emotions because in the end, it could be my downfall. I thought how Sergeant Rodriguez must have felt at the moment. He was probably feeling proud of himself. I had to accept the outcome of my actions, move on and just make better choices. That day, I made it my mission to straighten up my act and get my rank back. In the meantime, I would have to deal with the questions behind my new rank. Regardless of the looks and whispers, I was not going to let it get to me. I was going to keep my head held high and just move forward. Here we go.

Chapter 19

Bitter Sweet

Losing rank sucked though, however, being kicked off the mission was even worse. To add insult to injury, they made me catch a cab home. I was upset and relieved at the same time. Upset at the fact that I was no longer a part of the mission yet, relieved that now I would be able to see Kenniya and the girls, sooner than later. I called Kenniya to set up a day and time for her and the kids to come to NY. When the day came for me to see her, I was so stoked that I could hardly wait to wrap my arms around her and tell her how terrible it was to be away from her so long. Kenniya took a New Jersey bus to Times Square then she caught a cab to my sister's house. I was already outside waiting when I saw the car pull up. I smiled from ear to ear as I walked up to the vehicle. I greeted them with hugs and kisses that were long overdue. We unloaded her bags then headed upstairs, then once we got inside, I called my mother to see the baby. Since it was early in the afternoon, only my mother was home. Everyone else was at work or school so we stayed until the rest of my family arrived later that evening. After about three hours, I was ready to leave so I could have some quality time with them. Kenniya prepared the girls for our departure while I made arrangements for us to stay at a hotel suite. We called a cab and headed for the hotel room. As soon as we got inside, I grabbed Kenniya from behind, put her on the bed then pushed her against the wall, catching her off guard. Before she could say anything, I kissed her hard and fast, almost forgetting the kids were in the room too. *"The girls"* she managed to say through heavy breaths. "Oh yeah, my bad I said. I missed you so much". She replied, "I missed you too". Then she added "I had too many sleepless nights". I kissed her eyes as I always did when I knew she had been crying. I then said, "I'm here now". Later that night we put the kids in the room and Kenniya and I layed on the pull-out couch in the other room. My loins ached for her body so when she joined me in the bed, I kissed her all over while tugging at her clothes. She was just as "wanting" as I was. We were at each other hungrily, trying not to be too loud. I loved how Kenniya would grab my hands and rest it on her ass so that I could squeeze it. She loved her butt grabbed. I obliged by palming it, gripping it and spanking it a little. I went to get on top but she pushed me back so she could get on top herself. She stood up and smirked as she took off her clothes. I started to take off mine until she gestured for me to stop. Kenniya then took off my shirt, then my pants, kissing on me as she did it. She then kissed and licked my dick, making sure she looked at me as she teased me with her tongue. I watched as she proceeded to climb on top of me and start to gyrate in my lap in a seductive way. I went to put my erect dick in her however, she stopped me once again. She gave me a mischievous look and continued to grind allowing her juices to saturate my crotch. I went to feel her breasts and after stopping me again, I finally got the hint. She licked her lips and started to grind faster as I watched her supple breasts hover inches from my mouth. My tongue stuck out instinctively, trying to sample the goodness that was before it. This time, she didn't move. I was permitted to wrap my mouth around one of them before she quickly pulled away. I said, *"now you're playing"*. She replied, "so what are you going to do about it?" I quickly reversed positions, then grabbed both her wrists with one hand. I let my other hand dip in her honey pot. I let my fingers swim around as I watched her squirm beneath me. I took my fingers back out to examine the wetness that drenched my fingers. Then while looking in her eyes, I tasted each finger. She asked, *"how does it taste?"* Wanting her to find out herself, I stuck out my tongue, letting her lips completely envelope it. No longer being able to contain myself I penetrated her, pumping strong yet gentle. She had to cover her mouth, so her moans were muffled. I kept it up, diving as deep as I could, amused at her attempt to keep quiet. I kept it up until her body trembled, while I poured all my love into her. I collapsed on the side of her, muttering the words *"I love you"*. She said *"I love you more"* then we both passed out to what I thought would be a blissful sleep. Around 3:00am I woke up to the sound of sobbing and I instantly knew that it was the nightmares she mentioned. She sat up slowly then spoke softly between sobs and asked, *"why do you keep leaving me?"* I could not help but to tear up. I felt helpless though most of all, I felt responsible. Bringing her closer to me I said *"I will never leave your side"*, I spoke again saying *"time and distance may separate us but I'll always find my way back"*. I then kissed her tears, my lips lingering under each eye. She exhaled then nuzzled her nose in my chest. Kenniya stayed there with her face buried until she was fast asleep. For the rest of the night, I monitored her sleep. Although my eyes were closed, I listened carefully for any signs of a bad dream. Paying close attention to any jerking of the body, mumbling or any sniffles. Thank goodness her nightmare did not return. Once I read this article that stated that people need to be careful of what they see as well as listen to before and during bedtime. What we feed our minds can have an effect during our resting periods and even in our subconscious while we are awake. Taking that into consideration, I thought to catch Kenniya's nightmare before it started. Maybe if I reassured her and spoke to her while she slept it would change the nature of her dreams. So, the next night, I stayed up while Kenniya slept. Every now and again, I whispered in her ear saying, *"I love you and will never leave your side"*. Finally, after several hours I called it quits. Just when I thought to fall asleep myself, Kenniya started muttering inaudible words. While spooning her from behind, again I whispered, *"I love you and will never leave your side"*. I added *"I'm here, right here and here is where I remain"*. I was beyond relieved when her mumbling stopped. I never told her what I was doing or what I did. I just continued the process for the rest of the week until eventually her nightmares stopped. Thankfully enough, even when she went back to New Jersey, Kenniya's nightmares did not return. Now that was taken care of, it was back to trying to fix our living arrangements.

Chapter 20

A hard head makes a soft ass

It is said that time heals all but then again it can work against you. In my case it was the latter. I felt like the more time spent away from Kenniya the more distance there was between us. Don't get me wrong, we talked a lot, still Kenniya wanted more. She called me all the time complaining about her mother and how annoying she was. She would then say how she could not wait until she got out of her mother's house and that I needed to stop living in a Motel. Every now and again, she would ask me what progress I have made, if any. I would give the same answer in different ways. I'd say "no, not yet these things take time" or "I'm doing my best". Kenniya might have meant well nevertheless I still felt pressured and in turn started stressing. There was no way to speed things up, it wasn't like I could pull a rabbit out of a hat. New York was too expensive. I needed to go somewhere that gave me more for my buck. I considered leaving the state, so that meant a new car and new job. I needed to plan accordingly; she was just going to have to be patient. At least try to. The real challenge for me was remaining level headed during this difficult time. I needed an outlet to help me achieve that goal. I had to talk to someone, someone who would not judge me. The first person that came to mind was my homeboy, Warren. Back in the day my friends and I were always at his house. His mother was basically our second mother. I stayed in touch with him and his mother throughout the years, even stopping by the house every once in while so when I started coming around more often, they did not mind. I had to give it to him because not a lot of men were willing or even capable of listening to another man's problems, especially if the problems are dealing with emotions. Warren on the other hand, let me talk his ear off. For a while I was doing "ok".

Distracting myself with Black ops, weed, alcohol and entertainment. There was never a dull moment at Warren's house. If I wasn't around his family, then I would be around his friends or his neighbors. Still, from time to time, I'll have a moment where I'm "spaced out" thinking about Kenniya and the kids. I tried so hard to stay away from those moments though sometimes you can't help what comes to mind. It wasn't long before I went back to old habits...women. I was walking to the store when I saw this "bow legged" chocolate slim goodie with a booty. She was walking in my direction so all I had to do to get her attention was walk directly in front of her. Of Course, she looked at me like I had two heads nonetheless once I started laying it on "thick", she was all smiles. I gave her my number and watched her walk away. Later that evening I was back at Warren's house playing Black Ops. Kenniya called however; I decided that I would call her back because my "team" needed me. I called her as soon as the round was over. She answered excitedly. *"Hey"* she said. I responded, *"hey boo, I just finished playing Black Ops...How are you?"* She said, *"great actually but I have a question"*. I said, *"I should have an answer"*. She asked, *"do you love me?"* I answered with the utmost confidence, *"always and forever"*. She then asked, *"are you sure?"* I chuckled nervously and then said *"uuuhhh of course"*. My mind quickly started to think about what I could have done wrong that she would know. After coming up with nothing, I asked *"what's up?"* It is interesting how men get caught creeping. When she told me what she knew, I was flabbergasted. I could not fathom how I could have done this myself. If I was sure about anything in my life, I was sure that what I've done was the straw that broke the camel's back and that I lost her. Somehow, I gave Ms. Bow leg, Kenniya's number. See my first mistake was sharing a phone plan with Kenniya, the second was allowing our cell phone numbers to remain similar with only one number being different. The last of course was giving it out in the first place. You might say that I was just careless but I think it was along the lines of something divine. Either way I was busted and no matter what excuse I came up with, like "I took her number for my friend". Kenniya wasn't trying to hear it. For the rest of the night, I just sat and thought about how I allowed this to happen and how I was going to fix it. I sent her one long text apologizing but the only response I got was a link to a song "bad decisions" by Trey Songz. I played that song on repeat for about a week straight. I even made a playlist of sad songs to add to my sorrows. Boy oh boy was I in my feelings. Still, it was not as bad as all that came later...

Dedication

First and foremost, I would like to dedicate this book to GOD who has always been in the mist. Never allowing me to dig a hole so deep that I could not climb back out. For giving me grace and mercy. For blessing me with potential and the mind to see it within myself. I would like to thank the people I've met on my journey so far. Each of you has given me something that shaped me into the man I am today.

To my family who supported me in different ways, especially my mother, most of all who only wanted the best for me no matter my flaws.

To my old bestie, I thank you for your time, your ear and for being there when I needed you. You will forever be in my heart. J.R.C

Finally, to my friend who was there to see me fall, time and time again but never gave up on me. For pulling me out of the darkness that I welcomed, for holding me accountable and assisting me in being a better man. Shout out to Baltimore from which she hails.

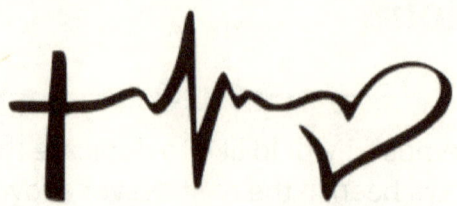

Like, Love or hate this book? Don't forget to leave a review and let me know your thoughts, feelings and opinions. Part 2 coming soon.

Every review matters so head over to Amazon and leave a comment for me. Please and thank you. Follow me on Tictok @Bishop3364 Email me bishop3364@yahoo.com

When we go through a traumatic situation, it effects us mentally and emotionally whether we like it or not. Mental health is so important. You can be physically fit, you can go to church, still if your not mentally healthy you can hurt a lot of people in your path, including yourself. Please seek therapy.

1 in 4 women and 1 in 7 men in the US experience rape, physical violence and/or stalking in their lifetime. 1 in 3 teens experience dating violence. Family and domestic violence is a common problem in the United States, affecting an estimated 10 million people every year.

Domestic violence is a serious issue and if you're experiencing it, talk to somebody immediately. The best thing you can do is seek professional help. Call toll free 1800-799-7233

www.ingramcontent.com/pod-product-compliance
Lightning Source LLC
Chambersburg PA
CBHW020705260626
47157CB00008B/3145